THE KENLEY CONUNDRUM

Donald Smith

Published by New Generation Publishing in 2024

Copyright © Donald Smith 2024

First Edition

The author asserts the moral right under the Copyright, Designs and Patents Act 1988 to be identified as the author of this work.

All Rights reserved. No part of this publication may be reproduced, stored in a retrieval system or transmitted, in any form or by any means without the prior consent of the author, nor be otherwise circulated in any form of binding or cover other than that which it is published and without a similar condition being imposed on the subsequent purchaser.

ISBN: 978-1-83563-347-2

www.newgeneration-publishing.com

New Generation Publishing

PROLOGUE

1945

Berlin.

Hitler's bunker.

A month before the Red Army arrived from the east.

Despite having clearly lost everything the Fuhrer was still ordering his generals to fight on.

He ate cakes voraciously.

His hands trembled.

The end was near but he kept preaching Victory. The high priest of mass murder was losing his mind. It was just three weeks before he would marry Eva Braun. Soon after he will poison them both and then shoot himself to be sure. Was it his chriptorchidism or injury in the Battle of the Somme that had driven him on? Maybe something else? The world will never know.

One matter of great importance required his immediate attention. Several years ago, when German power was at its height, his military leaders had presented him with an extraordinarily valuable amulet endorsing what he and they were all about. Taken from history and embellished a little. It was a silver diamond studded jewel with hints of the Black Sun. From a sideways view the keen observer could just make out the shimmering idea of a swastika. The amulet was to be worn around his neck.

It stood for good luck, success in all you do, it was symbolic of victory and spoke of overwhelming global leadership. Like amulets throughout the ages it was *known* to possess mystical qualities.

It would protect its wearer.

It had the strength to move mountains!

It was extraordinarily special to the cause.

His warped mind *knew* the fight had to go on. The amulet power and influence *must* continue. He tearfully returned it to its protective metal box very carefully.

There was no hesitation.

It had to be his long-serving manservant.

Fanatically loyal and a mature thirty-five years of age.

Totally convinced.

Prepared to fight to the death for the Fatherland, whatever the odds.

He sent for Abelard Schneider.

A couple of weeks later, and with the amulet unboxed and carefully contained in the heel of his left boot, Schneider retreated from the bunker and made his way to what was destined to become the British Sector of Berlin. Anything to get away from the Russians.

The intensity of the military surveillance there surprised him. They picked him up. Under questioning, and to save his own skin, he admitted that he spent some of his days in the bunker looking after the needs of his Supreme Leader. Red rag to a bull! Together with another soldier named Gunter Weber he was flown to England for interrogation.

The two shared a locked room in an old building. They became friends, keeping each other more or less sane in difficult circumstances. Weber had been involved in munitions production and the Brits wanted to know all about locations. Both were allowed out for exercise for limited periods only.

In a very short time the war had ended with German surrender in September 1945. They worked on with the British agricultural industry and were billeted on farms with minimal supervision. It was during this time, when he was alone, that Schneider decided to hide the amulet. He would be returned to his home country any time soon and he knew that it was under the full military control of the victors. He would again be investigated and they could well find his priceless treasure. Like Hitler he believed as an absolute certainty that the Nazis would rise again. Of course the Aryan race was superior to all others. It had to control once more, though the next time it would be wise to take the Brits with them.

He chose his day and made his way alone to his planned hiding place. There was nobody around. He extracted the amulet from his heel, returned it to its metal box which he had managed to retain, and hid it where he was sure it could not be found. Only then did he go back to the farm feeling much happier.

Several weeks later they were returned to their homeland. Before parting company Abelard Schneider gave Weber, whom he now considered to be his very close friend, some limited amulet detail about what would be of great importance to a future Nazi leader, and a convoluted sketch plan for finding it. Those who knew what they were looking for would be likely to understand the detail. As a confirmed Nazi he did not wish the amulet to be for ever lost if anything untoward should happen to him.

Weber was intrigued by the story he was told and accepted the explanatory design he was given. It had garbled information on it, the solution to which would lead to the whereabouts of the precious jewel. Any unknowing person, Brit, American, Russian, French or even German, probably unaware of the amulet's existence, would find the content completely meaningless and would bin it. Only a top surviving Nazi, and one would inevitably emerge, would have some understanding. They agreed to keep in touch and exchanged the likely addresses where each could be found in the future.

What Schneider did not know was that Weber had always been a dyed in the wool Communist with absolutely no sympathy at all for the Nazi cause. He had worked in munitions simply to comply with the vicious regime and protect his life. He had always held a deep down hatred for Hitler and all he stood for.

Arriving home, Schneider unsurprisingly found chaos all around. He was labelled a top Nazi. Life was extremely unpleasant. Like some others he fled, choosing to go to southern Africa where he had been told there were small but sympathetic German settlements and that living there would be somewhat less difficult.

Weber went to his home which was in the Russian sector. On the eighth of February 1950 the Ministerium fur Staatsicherheit or Stasi was formed. To many German citizens they were terrifying but to Weber they represented the future. As a fervent communist he went to see them. He saw it as his duty to pass on the sparse amulet information which he had received from Schneider.

ONE

Piet Geldenhuys dropped his briefcase and travel bag on to the hall table and made straight for the kitchen fridge. It was unbearably hot outside and a cool beer at the end of a very busy day had now become important. The past week had seen him visit three countries up north in quick succession. His reports back to London could wait. He sank back in to his most comfortable lounge chair, sipped the drink and pushed the television button. It was good to be home.

His small apartment in Pretoria was a lifeline. It was cool and friendly and suited his bachelor existence. He had been here for five years now, having moved in on his twenty-seventh birthday. Grace Chilungwe came in twice a week and helped out with the general running of the place. She was due in tomorrow. He used the small second bedroom as an office and would spend time there while she sorted things. The system worked well.

Piet was a director of MarketWorld, a London-based company situated near to the Thames Vauxhall Bridge. It had been formed over a year ago. His geographical remit was Africa. The whole of it. The marketing detail he was shortly to send off was good. He had found excellent sources of information in all the countries he had visited. This time David Johnston, on behalf of clients, was after information on three products - farm fertilisers, hair straightening devices and outboard engines for small boats. The idea was to look ahead and, by whatever means, to establish how future thinking was going. It was marketing research but done in much more detail than almost any of the international competition. World beating computer programming enabled London, using his survey details, to predict with unparalleled accuracy future requirements in selected countries for those products. He enjoyed the work, especially seeing and dealing with the different human reactions to his often wide-ranging questions.

The sun was beginning to go down and it was time to eat. He had noticed some biltong in the kitchen left there by the ever resourceful Grace. He wandered out to get it and at the same time managed to find some fruit. Dinner was frugal enough but he was not hungry. The airline had fed him well.

Soon it was news time. He returned to his seat and upped the volume. The usual problems were still being played out. Widespread corruption in South Africa. Lots of poverty around. The Chinese were pushing in the whole time and there were two or three strikes in some of the mines. He often wondered if those news people ever had anything good to pass on. He was about to turn off when an item of local interest made him sit up and pay close attention.

"Ringleader Sally Lenshina, assisted by French prisoner Marguerite Villeneuve, today orchestrated a riot in the Johannesburg Female Correction Centre. A dozen women refused to carry out their daily work, shouting at, and attacking, the prison warders. They said they were crowded into small rooms where it was very hot. The place was filthy. There were cockroaches, bedbugs and fleas everywhere. Standards were well below all rules concerning prisoner welfare. The police subsequently intervened and now all is quiet."

Piet knew what "police intervened" meant. Any number of women would now be nursing their wounds. Although they lived in a democratic country it still seemed that the authorities, and the police in particular, recognised few restraints. But it was the French woman's name which had really caught his attention.

Marguerite Villeneuve had to be the woman who was imprisoned over a year ago for theft. He had known her as Lady Banforth after he had tracked her to her manor home near Cambridge, England, only later learning of her French name on her conviction. Hearing the woman's name now opened up a whole historical can of worms in his mind. He hadn't really since thought about those criminals, of whom she was one, who had been put behind bars for long periods of time. Of course they were imprisoned in South Africa, having been caught and sent here from surrounding African countries where she and a fellow crook had been picked up trying to remain incognito whilst loaded down with stolen krugerrands. He switched off the television and made his way slowly into the bedroom.

Sleep came easily. He was tired out.

Then suddenly, at two in the morning, Piet jerked awake, his mind insisting on exploring past events. It was, inevitably, all about Marguerite Villeneuve. The old lady with the young heels. He had felt a bit of a fool at the time explaining to the others that he was a heels man. But it had been Marguerite who was staring at them that time outside the Bank of England. Also it was she he had seen sitting in a café at the end of Charles the Second Street in London with a large picture of David Johnston, his present day boss and friend, laid out on the table beside her coffee, quietly seeking him out.

What on earth made her tick? How had she come to be associated with her ex-Stasi boss Breck Haffenbacker? What did she really look like without her old lady disguise? That time in Wick, Scotland, he had seen her across the restaurant but only fleetingly. She must now have been held in jail for more than a year. What on earth would that do to her? She must feel incredibly lost. Probably frantic. Her native France and her adopted home in England were a long way off. And where was Haffenbacker locked up?

He rolled over and tried unsuccessfully to sleep.

How much of a prison sentence was she given? Probably a pretty long one - pinching the Pretoria Mint's wealth in such volumes was an awful crime. What did Haffenbacker get? After all he was the mastermind, having himself started the whole thing off. In a way Piet was glad he and his friends in London had failed to retain that wealth or they themselves could well now be serving time. But he really would like to know more, even if only to confirm things to his London colleagues.

He began to wonder. Maybe he should visit her? He knew that was possible despite some pretty rigorous rules. If he did what on earth would they find to discuss? Would her mind have remained sound in those awful confined and completely foreign conditions?

Something to think about, but it was probably a non-starter. He rolled over to face the other way, forced everything out of his mind, and went straight back into a deep sleep.

TWO

Early autumn, bright sunshine and a magnificent view out to sea. I was a very happy man. Lovely wife Elizabeth, beautiful son, Teddy, now aged two, a house in Hove and this Saturday morning I was free to walk to Brighton marina. There were a few swimmers in sight, though October seemed a little late for that, three small motor boats, one sailing yacht and, on the horizon, a huge freight vessel. The modest sized waves rolled gently up the pebble beach and then retreated uttering contented gurgling sounds all the way back down to the deep.

It all seemed a long way from the events of a couple of years ago, the trauma of which had cemented our relationships for life. All four of us had formed MarketWorld and, despite the usual competitive market forces, the company had gone from strength to strength. The one disadvantage of living in Hove was the commuting to the London office, but we had minimised the effect of that by retaining Elizabeth's flat in Pimlico and frequently staying over.

I was still amazed that she had gone through with it and married me after the South African Mint theft business had been sorted out. True to her suggestion our honeymoon had been on a cruise ship which called in to Flaam in Norway where she presented her contact there, Mrs Ericsson, with a krugerrand necklace, and at the same time explained how it was that her son had recovered his repaired boat at no cost. It was a long and involved story which she had reduced to a few sentences. We parted the very best of friends.

The seagulls were circling around the end of Brighton pier, a sure sign that there were fish around. I think we now had to call them gulls though I'm not sure why. The traffic was beginning to build, indicating that the weather forecast had been good. Although Brighton and Hove were now an item, Hove still clung fervently to its considerably more up-market image. Visitors would always swarm to the Brighton pier and surrounding beach. Hove received slightly less attention and we'd chosen well. We had to make the most of the weekend as on Monday I would be joining the mad rush for the London-bound train and then an important meeting with Global Incorporated, our most celebrated customer.

I walked briskly on to the marina which looked to be getting busy. People were taking out their boats for a final trip before the winter really set in. From a distance I had a quick look at our boat, named Thor. All seemed well with her. Elizabeth and I had come all the way across the sea from Bergen to Wick in Scotland in *that!* We must have been mad, despite the fact that she was a seasoned yachtmaster.

I checked my watch and turned quickly around. It was some way back and I was very shortly due to meet her and Teddy at the Pier for his first ever outing there.

THREE

For most of the next morning Piet's mind kept coming back to the idea of visiting the female prison. The idea was a tricky one to put it mildly. He had never actually met Marguerite, although David and Elizabeth had. At the point of her gun! They would be none too pleased with him. To them she was a nasty and violent enemy.

On the other hand he was curious. A youngish French woman held in a crowded South African jail. It would be very hot in the daytime and clearly, according to the television news, she was causing trouble because of the conditions. The whole thing did make him wonder. All the reports about her from the others had reckoned she was highly intelligent and positive in all that she did, although from their viewpoint she was totally destructive also.

Maybe ask David in London what he thought?

He quickly dismissed that one. His friend would almost certainly not like the idea. Right down deep he was feeling increasingly strong rumblings that he himself should do a visit to the woman if that were at all possible. She might refuse to see him, but if they did meet he would learn more about all that had gone on from her viewpoint. After all, the whole thing was over now and those on her side were very much the losers. Given a different scenario he and his friends could themselves be doing time. A short chat with her could do no harm, could it?

One of the biggest problems might be to get her to agree to see him. Just how should he describe himself to her, maybe through a third party at the prison? The rules about prison visits stated that her agreement to any meeting was imperative.

He had considered discussing the whole matter with Grace who had been in for the morning and was now gone, but he had quickly dismissed the idea because, given the history of the whole matter, it would have been difficult to know where to begin. Once he started on the story of Elias Mubanga's death and the whole krugerrand saga he would have had to tell her everything about their own dodgy activities, and that he was not prepared to do. The four of them had agreed that they must for ever keep quiet about their role in chasing the hidden krugerrands.

He was out on his own. Visit or no visit? He sat down at the computer which he had already briefly consulted. He would follow up on the precise detail of the visitation process.

FOUR

Things were working out well. I was having an off the cuff meeting with Walt Denison, Global's new director of marketing.

"Sure you won't re-join us? We could make things very worthwhile." He hinted at the same thing whenever we met. This time it was a positive request.

"No, sorry Walt. The answer is still the same. The unanimous view of our directors is that for us small is beautiful. And these days MarketWorld does have other clients - much leaner ones than you of course." Next month I had two major appointments in the West Country with new companies wanting to use our services and I knew Jonny had half a dozen to visit up north.

Coffee arrived.

Bone china cups.

Exotic silver tray and spoons.

Biscuits to die for.

This was not quite like the old days when I had worked here before we were bought out by them. Walt poured. I looked around the thirtieth floor boardroom. They had changed a couple of wall hanging pictures to give an American feel to the place, but the rosewood table at which we sat and its matching comfortable chairs remained. The commanding view out over Vauxhall London had been ruined by the erection of a large number of T-cranes which we were told were revitalising building works post Covid.

"How's Elizabeth?"

He had known her from the days of the takeover. Several years previously I had persuaded her to leave Harley Street and join my department in Armstrong and Acherson as a marketing analyst - long before the Yanks, in the form of Global, had arrived.

"She's fine thanks."

"And Teddy?"

"Two years old tomorrow. Full of fun."

I took a little milk. "How is your family surviving the London life, Walt?"

"Just fine. The move from Connecticut has turned out well. And of course we go back to see the folks fairly often." He looked me firmly in the eye. I wondered what was coming as he had specially requested that I pop in to see him.

"At our board meeting last week it was agreed that my plans for setting up Global distribution centres in Singapore and South Africa be implemented. All the strands of our activities in Asia and Africa would have local control from those two places. Pure logic really."

"Sounds good." I nodded my head in appreciation.

"We really do like the efforts of your man in Africa as you know. Any chance of you putting something similar in to Singapore or somewhere in that rapidly expanding area?"

He sugared his coffee and slowly stirred.

I thought quickly. Piet Geldenhuys in Pretoria was doing us and them a wonderful job. We would have to find someone of similar calibre for the Asian work. Not easy.

"We might help financially with the initial costs."

They were clearly enthusiastic.

"I need to consider, Walt. This is very sudden."

"We are under pressure to expand in Asia. That is *the* major upcoming area of business activity right now and for the foreseeable future. We need your particular expertise. Your African market investigations still frequently produce results which we really like."

"We have a board meeting coming up next week. I wouldn't envisage any problem but it is a big step for us. I could come and see you to discuss detail after that?"

"Fine, David. I will email our ideas to you. Our whole company is pressing so make it quick."

I finished the coffee and stood up. He was an extraordinarily busy man. We shook hands. I took a final look out across London as I swung around to the exit door and made for the lifts. Our small strategically positioned offices were just a ten minute walk away.

FIVE

"Passport."

Piet handed it over. The man studied it. Then him. He passed it back. It was a match.

"Stand up straight please."

Piet obliged. And was thoroughly frisked.

"You may sit."

Piet sat.

A phone conversation then took place which he could not fully hear in a language he did not completely understand. He spoke Ndebele and Afrikaans but it was neither of these. He stared around at the white ceiling and austere furnishings. The windows were barred and there seemed to be cctv everywhere.

God, how awful.

Before long a blue uniformed warder appeared. She looked at the warden and said simply, "Yes, ok."

He rose, pinned an already prepared visitor tag to Piet's shirt pocket, and indicated that he should follow her. They passed a small tuck shop where Piet had understood from the blurb he had previously read that he might later be allowed to buy a delicacy for the prisoner. Then they entered a friendless room whose only furniture comprised two uncomfortable wooden chairs which were positioned facing each other. She went off leaving him standing and listening to mother and child noises echoing around this part of the building.

He sat down on one of the chairs. It seemed the obvious thing to do. This room was even more boring than what he had so far seen of the rest of the building. Nothing. Just nothing except two chairs and heavily barred windows. One had to struggle just to see the sky. He was becoming nervous. Gone was the positive feeling about seeing inside one of these places. It was a conscious decision, although a bit impetuous, to come here but he was now wondering.

No more time to think. Footsteps sounded and he stood up. The warder returned with Marguerite in tow and indicated to them both to sit, she herself remaining within hearing distance.

Piet was horrified at what confronted him. He again recalled having seen this woman at a distance in that hotel in Wick. As far as he could remember she had been very well turned out, indeed handsome with it. Now she was thinner, ashen faced, with a couple of nasty looking arm bruises on view. She had an all-over resigned appearance. She was ready to give in. Maybe had already thrown in the towel. The system had knocked the stuffing out of her and he was not at all surprised at that!

"I can get you something to eat?" That seemed an easy start and she did look as if she needed sustenance rather badly.

"Yes please! A chocolate bar. I know they do them but I have never before had a visitor."

Piet thought about that. A whole year shut off in this place, or somewhere similar, completely isolated from the outside world. The warder had a duty to remain in earshot but when Piet produced a substantial note she offered to carry out the purchase for him. As soon as she had left Marguerite snapped out of her "all is lost" mode and whispered hurriedly at him.

"You *must* get me out of here if I am to live. I am slowly dying. *Please, please* help me! I have nobody else."

"You were our enemy! And you want my help? I came here for a chat, nothing else."

"Yes, yes. I guess you did. I will repay you all somehow. That was a long time ago. I *must* escape. I am beaten, kicked and spat at. All day. Every day. I have no contact with England or France or anywhere! Nobody knows I am here. If I cannot get out soon I will just die." The tears were streaming down her dishevelled face giving her an even worse appearance.

At that moment the chocolate arrived. They were given a bar each but no change was offered back to Piet, and no way was he going to ask.

Marguerite managed a slight change of tone.

"Oo, thank you Piet. This is lovely."

"My pleasure."

"We really must do this again. I would like to see you and talk more about things." She closed her eyes, apparently in deep thought.

"What sort of things, Marguerite?"

"Beaches where you can swim. Wide open spaces. Hills. Valleys. I dream of these things. Above all, motor cars. Short journeys. I love them. Haven't seen one for a whole year."

The warder was pacing the room and occasionally walking outside and just out of earshot presumably to alleviate her boredom. She had done this so often and the duty was pretty humdrum.

While she was at that distance Piet spoke very quietly.

"Motor car? What about it?"

"A hundred metres down the road. I could escape in it." She pointed in the direction it should face.

"But you *can't* get out of here!"

"I *can*. Got it all worked out. I just need the chance. This incarceration is not human. Next visit can you talk dates and please be ready for me?" She was whispering very quietly. Piet could only just make it out. "It really will be worth your while. I have big secrets to share with you - to make up for the past."

The woman came back in. That conversation came to an abrupt end.

They turned their thoughts to other subjects. How was she getting on? How long to go on her sentence? Piet knew it was huge. Could he bring her anything in particular during his next visit? Time ran out very quickly. Piet said he would try and visit again the following Tuesday - in exactly a week's time. He knew that was permitted in their rules. He then waited whilst she was escorted back to her cell.

The warder quickly returned and ushered him out, the whites of her eyes shining intensely out of her black face as she tried to puzzle out precisely why a nice guy like this could have the slightest interest in such a desperately troublesome and unstable inmate.

SIX

Piet often ate out in the evening but now needed quiet time at home alone to mull over all he had learned during his visit. What he had found was partly expected. But there were areas of the whole scenario which he needed to explore in detail.

To some extent Marguerite's shocking demeanour was not surprising. She was an up-market French woman held in a South African jail with people most of whose customs and languages were completely foreign to her.

He was very aware from past experience that she had been a tough operator in the search for those elusive krugerrands. She had backed her partner, Herr Haffenbacker, to the hilt, and had been an absolute thorn in the side of David and Elizabeth - well all four of the team really.

He munched his supermarket steak ready meal without really tasting it. The woman was getting the treatment she deserved. She had jilted her husband, Lord Banforth, in the most shocking way, though to be fair the noble Lord himself did not seem to be at all interested in fighting her cause. He was nowhere to be seen and seemed to have left her to rot. So maybe there was nothing in their betrothal anyway. She had played really rough when she and Haffenbacker broke into Elizabeth's place in Pimlico, holding her at gunpoint. And she was a thief and had rightfully been imprisoned for it. However, to be fair, Piet and his three friends had also been thieves. They were beaten at the last hurdle and had lost most, though not all, of the loot, thereby avoiding legal repercussions being aimed at themselves.

Should he discuss with David what to do? Help her or not? Simply aid her escape? The answer coming back from London would almost certainly be negative. They had all been put through just too much pain. There was no way that David, Elizabeth and Jonny could find a modicum of the goodwill which was required to forgive. He felt sure of that. All three of them had been so very badly treated.

He would have to make up his own mind.

What he had seen made him feel enormous sympathy for the plight in which Marguerite now found herself. He knew her sentence was a very long one - being caught with huge amounts of South African Mint wealth had inevitably led to a massive punishment. Thank God they themselves had not succeeded. For him personally simply to shrug his shoulders and leave her to her fate felt wrong. Should he just walk away? Leave her to suffer? Let her live with her punishment?

His problem was that when on the spot he had seen with his own eyes the complete mess she was in. He completely believed what she was saying. She *would* die! And quite soon too the way things were. Being condemned to death in this way was too great a punishment for the crime committed. But was *he* in any position to set *himself* up as judge and jury?

He left most of the meal, stood up, and started to pace the room. He was on his own on this one. Nobody else would understand her awful predicament. The devastation of that one human being's life was palpable. She had not been sentenced to death, or anything like it, but that would be the inevitable result.

And soon.

What was the minimum he could do to help her? Her request seemed to have been for transport. He had promised her another visit. He was her only contact with anything that must in the slightest way seem to her to be *sane*. Maybe there was such a thing as honour amongst thieves. He could not live with himself if she were to die on his watch. He would not tell the others in London but he had now convinced himself that he would visit her again and try to help out in some way.

SEVEN

Incarceration in this place did not feel so final that night. It seemed that there was a chance.

A slim one.

Just a chink of light.

But a chance.

She *had* to get out. Die in the attempt if necessary. She was sufficiently well trained to do it. As a graduate of the French Direction-General de la Securite Interieur she felt equipped both mentally and physically to deal with most situations. But this imprisonment had shaken her self-belief. One whole year and she was still locked up and steadily losing the will to live.

"When the smallest opportunity occurs grab it with both hands. Wait! Plan! Pounce!"

This tenet of her teaching was one of many which had been instilled into her very being. She was now thirty one years of age. At her peak, but nearing total exhaustion.

Her visitor! Her enemy competitor had come in to see her! He knew the score. He, too, had been one of life's chancers. One of the four of them. They had not succeeded in laying hands on those krugerrands. She had. And had landed up here.

Why had he come to see her? It certainly wasn't to gloat. She could see the horror he felt at her situation oozing out from his very pores. He had been aghast at the sheer nothingness of the place. The man felt for her. There was a chance!

She felt the old cunning very slowly coming back. She had long calculated that actually exiting this prison was possible. But once outside she was running blind. She knew France. She understood Britain. Anywhere in Europe she could get by. But to be moneyless in the streets of completely unknown Johannesburg was lethal. She badly needed a point of contact. The old "Daggers" organisation was no more and Haffenbacker, her old boss, was held in a very secure place for a much longer term even than hers. There was just one member who was still at large in South Africa who might help her - if she could find him. The minimum requirement to survive was a car. She could live in that. Somehow she could find a way to move around, to steal petrol, food, clothing and other necessaries while she found the way to get out of the country. Anywhere would do. Any other country which would not be looking for her.

She slowly turned over, knowing she would not sleep. He had said he would come again in a week. She must be ready. Her present day job was making uniforms. She had learned how to disguise herself in her Paris days. Her work bag, where she kept bits and pieces of material, would become a repository for Escape Day. They never looked there. Difficult. But possible!

He *must* come!

EIGHT

One week later Piet visited.

Reception was the same. The robot of a man acted just as he had previously. The same woman collected him and led the way to the meeting room. He noted that the refreshment area was open as before. The awful background shouting and screaming noise still carried on. He sat himself down in one of the two ramshackle chairs still standing alone in that otherwise naked room. In minutes a miserable looking Marguerite Villeneuve slouched in and, at the instruction of the woman warder, lowered herself slowly into the other seat.

"Thank you, Piet, for coming." She said it quietly as if in a dream.

"A pleasure, Marguerite, you really do need some contact."

They went on talking sweet nothings for a while until he asked if she would like a little chocolate as before, or maybe something different.

"Yes please. The chocolate would be wonderful. And a coffee. I think that might be possible."

The underpaid lady warder looked hopeful as Piet passed her substantial cash as the last time. She bounced happily off to arrange delivery of the two items.

Piet kept his voice down. "I *am* prepared to help you despite the awful past. Just tell me what is best?"

Marguerite's eyes lit up. She had had plenty of time to think through everything and became instantly positive.

"There must be a car outside. Night time, ten to ten-thirty. Exactly one week today. False number plates? Ignition keys in it. Will pay you back."

"Where will you go?"

"I do not know but I *must* get out of here."

Piet made a mad on the spot decision.

"I will have to drive you initially. Talk then about where you go."

"Ok, thanks. Please just make sure you are there."

"Right. Understood."

The coffee and chocolate arrived back, but, as before, what had to be a substantial amount of change was not forthcoming. They continued chatting about nothing. The half-hour was soon up. Piet wished her all the best and said loudly and firmly that he could not come again for at least a month. She beseeched him to return as soon as he could as she was being escorted off.

He then left in the usual way wondering why on earth he had made such a bloody silly impulsive offer.

NINE

The email from Walt was as I had expected. Clear, precise and full of possibilities for us. I sent a copy to Elizabeth who was at home down in Hove looking after Teddy, and to Jonny, comfortably at work in the adjacent office. He came quickly in, bubbling with excitement.

"So they want us to establish another Piet. Same sort of work but in Singapore."

"Yes."

"You agreed to it?"

"Not just yet Jonny. That is quite a tricky area to stake out. Remember Piet has always lived in Africa. He takes in the sunshine, knows wild animals, snakes and all that, is aware the seasons and the various peoples in those markets. How on earth do we find someone with that same pedigree, but for a completely different part of the world?"

"What about adverts here and in the Singaporean press? But I guess you had better put that to Elizabeth!"

My wife was jealously guarding her Human Resources title and continuing to work hard for the company despite assiduously mothering Teddy at the same time. "Yep, I'll do that. I'm pretty sure she will ultimately come up with the right person, but it may take time."

At that moment our new staff member joined us. Three months ago we realised that a jack-of-all-trades administrative officer was necessary. My senior manager with Armstrong and Acherson (now American Global) happily joined us and had moved effortlessly in to the job. Giles Rathbury knew just about everything to do with office routines.

"Something's going on." His antennae never ceased working.

"We're looking for someone with full knowledge of Singapore to move in to that area and do a Geldenhuys there. Global want us to get moving on it. Any ideas?"

"I'll think about it. So we're expanding?"

"Maybe, but only if we can set it up really well. We have no slack on this one. A really good replica of Piet or nothing."

"Piet may have some ideas. He meets a lot of people engaged in work similar to his."

Giles prompted my memory. "He will not be coming to next week's board meeting. Something's come up. I had an email a couple of hours ago."

Jonny looked at me quizzically. "Unlike Piet. He's always keen to come over, if only to cash in another kruger or two. Must be important."

"Yes. Our meeting will go ahead anyway and I will send the requirement details to Piet in case he has any input to offer. We must deal urgently with Global's request. Elizabeth will, of course, be present."

The two of them went speedily off and I returned to the day's desk work. I reckoned the personnel solution would come ultimately from Elizabeth.

It was, quite simply, her cup of tea.

TEN

Tuesday week.

The day had arrived.

Marguerite and most of the others were heavily engaged with their uniform-making late that afternoon. But this time the near-empty workbag which she always carried back to her lonely cell afterwards would contain something unusual over and above the tissues, nail file and comb which were standard items. They never checked. There was no point as there wasn't anything anywhere which was worthy of being stolen.

The excitement in her mounted as the bell sounded and they rose and made their way back into their nightly imprisonment. She threw herself down on to her uncomfortable bed in the usual way. It was of the utmost importance that everything should appear to be boringly normal. She lay there for a couple of hours apparently resting from her heavy day's work, but in fact her mind was rigorously examining the plan. Towards the end of that time the usual awful food and drink was handed through the cell door bars. She ate and drank it all with unusual relish. Anything for stamina and strength. She was embarking on something enormous and had no idea what the next few hours would deliver. The adrenalin was flowing and she knew she had to maximise her food intake.

Yet again her mind went over everything. Was her plan missing something? It simply *must* work. And Piet Geldenhuys *had* to be there as promised. Her training had been detailed and was geared to cover almost any situation. But not this! She allowed herself a wry smile as she pictured her tutors in Paris. How on earth would they react to the problem she faced at the moment? With rigour and great care, of course.

In no time at all the bell went for nine o'clock. There was to be no noise from then onwards until six in the morning. Fortunately for her the faint light in the outside corridor stayed on all night. It was just enough to see by. Her time to start the great gamble had arrived.

She very quietly gathered together all the scraps of paper she had acquired and hidden over the past week and put them in a heap on the floor. She then darkened her face with some horrid old oil she scraped from the cell door hinges. Her bag lay on the floor. She opened it and pulled out one stolen blue coloured pair of trousers which she had kept for herself whilst cutting and sewing warder uniforms that afternoon. She wriggled into them over her prison clothing, taking her time and doing everything carefully.

All this while her mental clock was ticking. She could gauge her timing to within a minute. Still ten minutes to go. She had worked it all out. At a quarter to ten the balloon must really go up. The two matches! She tore open her thin mattress and pulled out the cardboard pocket matches she had managed to steal from a cigarette smoking prison inspector when he visited a few days ago.

She waited.
And waited.
The minutes ticked away.
Then it was time!

There was nobody around outside her cell. She struck the first match and set light to the dry scraps of paper. Then she carefully pulled her thin bed blanket over and placed it gently on top of the flames. Thick smoke immediately billowed everywhere. It took only half a minute for an angry fire alarm to go off. The deafening noise rang out. The set drill, instilled into the night shift warders in the event of fire, was immediately followed. They had to get the prisoners out into the compound and hold them there while the fire rescue people arrived and went about their jobs.

Marguerite was seen by a passing warder lying on her bed apparently overcome by smoke. She quickly unlocked the grilled door, rushed in and bent over the still body, realising too late that the smoke was actually coming from this cell. It was her last act for a while. Marguerite punch-chopped her as she had been taught long ago and dragged the unconscious body into an area of shadow from which it could not readily be seen. She extracted the woman's hat from her epaulette, pulled it down over her head to ear level and then ripped the blouse from her inert body and hastily put it on. White top, blue trousers, standard issue hat and black face. In this panic situation her disguise might just work.

No! It *had* to work!

She went out and joined the general rush going towards the outside compound but at the last minute Marguerite veered off in the direction of Reception. The fire people were just entering that way and she helpfully pointed them towards the fire, at the same time passing through their ranks and straight out into the dark night.

It was a mere twenty paces down to the main road. She moved quickly away to the right. A car! Any car? *There was one along there*. A parked car. It was the only one and was some fifty steps away. She hurried along and with no hesitation got in.

Piet did not recognise her. A black prison warder in uniform! Until she barked at him.

"Drive, drive, just go! Get me out of here!"

ELEVEN

Piet drove off at a steady speed in order not to attract attention. There was little traffic at that time of night and the fewer passers-by there were the better. He was now becoming increasingly worried about his own dangerous position in this whole affair.

"Where to?"

She had no answer to that.

"I don't know. I simply must not go back in there." She tossed her head backwards. "It will take them about two hours to discover everything I have done. Then they will go through the records and see that I have very recently had a visitor. They will be chez vous one hour after that. You, quite simply, must know nothing."

"Right. Understood. In the meantime what about you?"

"May I borrow some money? I will return it with interest. A largish hotel somewhere from where I can seek out my one contact here who could help me?"

Piet had anticipated this and handed over a bunch of notes. "Most people still do use money so that should see you through for a short time."

"Thanks Piet, a lot. I suppose you do not know where I could find some sort of female clothing - just enough to get me in to the hotel. I cannot appear anywhere in this outfit! Later I can shop."

"They will probably recognise you anywhere."

"No, not at all. I am now Jessica Rees-Morgan. I can become a different person very quickly and if I can find my contact I will be able to acquire a passport. He is in hiding - frightened for his life, I'm sure."

Piet put his foot down. He had now to move quickly to get her off his hands.

"Tissues to get that stuff off your face - open up in front of you."

"Ok, female clothing. The only thing I can think of right now is my home help who has a spare dress she keeps there for any "posh" event which may occur. They are very few and far between. You could try that. I can invent a reason for its loss and buy her something new."

She continued using up his tissues at a very fast rate as she spoke. "Sounds wonderful. Do you have a bathroom?"

Piet smiled as he recalled the jail conditions she had endured for such a long time. "You can have one hour in the bathroom. Unlimited hot water and soap, towels and even men's aftershave if you wish. While you do that I will book you in as Jessica Morgan, just arrived from the UK. I would suggest a faceless airport hotel."

"Jessica *Rees*-Morgan please!"

"Sorry, of course."

They had arrived.

Piet pushed a button and the garage door opened up. He drove straight in, closing the door behind them. He then led her out through the garage and into his flat, quickly closing the door. It was important that she should not be seen or even heard.

"Food or bath first?"

She was in no doubt.

"Definitely bath please."

He found Grace's dress and a large towel and pointed the way. Then he started to cook a chicken curry and laid two places at the small table. A bottle of red rounded it off. She could at least have a decent meal before she was off his hands.

It was all of one hour before she emerged from his small bathroom. Piet simply could not believe his eyes. The slightly ill-fitting dress did nothing to hide the shapely body beneath it and the oil-stained face had turned into something handsome. Her hair had been washed and done up magnificently. She was, indeed, a totally different person.

"Unrecognisable. You are beautiful, Marguerite. Sorry, I mean Jessica!"

As Marguerite Villeneuve in one country and Lady Banforth in the other she had found most men in France and the UK to be mere wimps when the chips were down. This man who had rescued her was certainly not one of them. He now had plenty to be worried about, but was not showing it.

"It feels really good to be out of that place. I could not have gone on much longer. You can have no idea just how wonderful was that bath. I've had nothing like it for a whole year."

Piet looked at his watch. "One and a half hours nearly gone. Come and eat. I hope you like curry?"

"I love it and the smell is gorgeous." She looked around the room. She was free. Truly free! It just had to stay that way.

"South African red?"

"Oh my god! Yes please. I haven't had a drink like that for a whole year either!"

"Well enjoy it. You have a tricky path ahead. I have booked you in to the largest Airport hotel. Late evening arrivals are not a problem for them. You are on your own after that."

"You know, Piet, this is making me very sorry that we behaved so badly towards you and your friends. There is no excuse. I was trained that way in France and linked up with Haffenbacker and the team as I fitted like a glove their requirements in London. Mainly Hatton Garden and all that. The Krugerrands business changed us from tough business people into criminals. Then, of course, we lost everything."

"Jessica, I really don't think we were much better. And one very deep secret for you. We did not come away with nothing. Not a lot, but not nothing!"

"Good. I'm glad you made a few krugers out of that awful time." She gave him a very straight look. "I am sorry I will not be meeting you again. There's a lot to talk about."

Piet felt the same. Rather strongly. He chose his words carefully.

"Well I know the hotel number and I know which name you will be using. So we might meet up in a few days time if you are still there. You will probably by then need another kruger's worth of my cash before you have everything sorted. Coffee coming up and then we *really must go*."

TWELVE

Karl Winkler lived alone in a small house near to the city centre in Walvis Bay, the great tourist attraction of Namibia. There was no real view out and it was a bit small but Karl had always lived here. He was now a retired seventy-one year old man whose wife had passed away some six years ago. Soon after her death he withdrew from his half century of work in the fishing industry. His two sons had left home many years ago, seemingly happy to get into the outside world, one to work in America and the other in the copper mines of the Democratic Republic of Congo. Meeting up with either of them had become a very rare event.

He had organised his life, in what to him seemed the only possible way in the circumstances, by keeping in touch with a couple of organisations which gave some meaning to his lonely existence. The most important of these comprised a small group of people, mainly of South African origin, some of whom were descendants of the friends and colleagues of the infamous Fritz Joubert Duquesne, born in Cape Colony, who, amongst other pro-German war activities, had headed up a Nazi spy ring of some thirty-three members.

The meetings, which took place monthly, had a homely but slightly clandestine feel to them. Clandestine because over the years both German and Afrikaans languages had attracted a sort of "colonial" feel about them. He himself had a German father who said that in his youth he had spent two years looking after the Fuhrer. He had fled to Walvis Bay after the

Second World War, where he had met and married his South African wife.

Although when they first arrived at a meeting the members would in the main speak English, there would always be a gradual slide into German, which he spoke fairly fluently. The meals they prepared were invariably a rouladen, sauerbraten or one of the many types of wurst. All followed by an apfelstrudel or something similar and washed down with copious amounts of German beer. He loved the whole thing as it reminded him of his father. Attendance at these gatherings had given a second home to him.

He also belonged to a club whose membership was restricted to retired workers from the fishing industry. Fishing was one of the main local activities and Karl had spent his life working in and developing a part of that business. He had watched it grow to the colossus it now had become. They were a very friendly lot, competitive rivalries subdued or forgotten with the arrival of old age. In this organisation fish was invariably on the menu!

Most days he would walk a lot. Across the salt flats, or down to view the dolphins and flamingos which he always hoped were around. If there was a cruise liner visiting he would go and have a look. And watching the activity of those container ships arriving at the modern terminal seemed almost unreal. He was fascinated by such developments which brought his home right into the modern era. When he really needed a change he would take the train inland to Windhoek where his father had often visited - this was for him still a real adventure.

These days he felt himself elderly but basically fit, happily retired, well pensioned and surrounded by friends who were not too intrusive.

Who, when all was said and done, could ask for more.

THIRTEEN

The meeting went ahead two days later. Elizabeth came up at mid-day from Hove, leaving Teddy in the care of her mother who had arrived from Worthing. She insisted on making "proper" coffee before we began.

I kicked off rather lamely.

"I have no suggestions to put forward. A Singapore Piet could be a great problem to find."

"Me too. I know a CBI man who covers that area but he's a bit civil servantish. And he probably earns a bomb there anyway. Well, way above the sort of pittance we might offer!"

Jonny shrugged his shoulders and looked hopefully at Elizabeth.

She smiled, and then didn't hold back. Once again she could prove to them that she was the woman for the job

"After huge investigation and talking to quite a few, I think I may have the person. Actually it is a team arrangement, man and wife. No children. Hongkongers who moved to London and took up British citizenship several months ago. They had spent three years living in Singapore working for a huge Chinese corporation. They are familiar with the ways of life there and would have no residence problems, certainly for a limited time."

"Does he, or they, know our type of work?" Jonny knew just how much of a rarity we were.

"Marketing planning they know a lot about - Hong Kong style. They could even have one or two things to teach us. But basically they are highly skilled and young enough to fit in to our ways. I asked them down to Hove and we had an almost instant meeting of the minds. They could well be what we are looking for."

So great was Elizabeth's wish to continue working - but from home yet keeping it out of home - that I, her closest person on this earth, had no inkling of what she had been up to.

I looked around. They were all keen to go ahead.

I finalised things right away.

"Giles, could you fix an appointment for them here please? Make sure we can all attend. Leave out Piet. He will not be over for a while. Reading between the lines it seems to me he's up to something. Great shame as he is key to the whole project."

FOURTEEN

They fixed things so that their arrival at the airport Protea hotel was at one in the morning. There were not many people around and, anyway, Piet was sure that Jessica was now unrecognisable, such was the change in her appearance that had taken place. Marguerite had definitely become Jessica!

They said their goodbyes quickly and she strutted confidently into the hotel, near empty case in hand. Reception were expecting her and handed over the access key immediately. Once safely locked into her second floor room she flung herself down on to on the bed and tried hard to drain away the tension she was feeling. She stared at the white ceiling. Then her eyes followed the walls around the room. She still couldn't believe it. She was safe! She was free!

Almost immediately she was up on her feet again. Coffee and tea - there was a plentiful supply. She checked the fridge - yes, drinks were there. Eating would be no problem as she could order food from room service. She cast an eye over the menus. They seemed truly amazing. And the bathroom - simply out of this world. No need to stick her head above the parapet for some time. She had a firm and safe base for several days.

She took off the ill-fitting dress and rested it carefully across a chair. Although desperately tired she simply could not resist taking another bath. There were so many goodies around - soap, shampoos, body lotions, slippers, a hair dryer and beautiful thick towels.

Half an hour later she walked back into the bedroom clothed only in a hotel dressing gown, lay down in the luxurious bed and pulled up the sheet and blanket. She put out the light and was asleep in seconds.

The following morning when Jessica awoke sunlight was streaming through chinks in the curtains. No sudden bright light and noise demanding that she jump up at six. She looked at the time winking at her from the base of the TV set. It was just after ten o'clock!

Sadly, in her heart, she knew it was now time to become real. She phoned down and asked for the standard breakfast to be delivered to her room. Then she washed and dressed in the only clothing she had. A trolley duly arrived. She sat at the small table, breakfast in front of her, a hotel note pad, pencil and map of Johannesburg on one side and coffee on the other. It was time to plan. Her French training was forcing its way to the front of her mind. This day she really had to act. Her survival depended on it.

FIFTEEN

Jessica left her room, put up the "Do not disturb" sign on the door, walked downstairs and straight out through the main entrance. She quickly found a taxi and asked to be taken to the much publicised Park Meadows shopping centre. Once there she settled the fare, looked around, was amazed at all that she saw, and went straight to the nearby ladies dress boutique.

Her first priority was a hat. She chose one large enough to protect her from the sun but which also served to hide her facial profile a little. She moved on to look at, and then buy, a pair of trousers, a blouse and an attractive jumper. And then a raincoat followed by two sets of underclothes. After purchasing a substantial bag in which to hold it all at checkout she moved on to a nearby shoe centre.

One comfortable pair of shoes later she looked carefully around for the most important shop of all - one which could provide a whole range of make-up items. Here she really enjoyed herself, having been highly trained about disguise in its many forms. This was so important now. She bought lipsticks, foundation, highlighters and shaders, mascara and eye shadow, hair pieces and hair dyes, nail varnish, a comb, toothbrush and paste and put them all into her bag as she left. In the taxi back to the hotel she felt just a tinge of guilt at the rapid depletion of Piet's money.

She carried her purchases quickly up to her room and set about the agreeable job of making herself as different as possible from the person who had been incarcerated in that awful place. She kept the old dress hanging in the wardrobe together with anything she was not immediately using. At the end of an hour's concentrated but enjoyably work she stood back and stared into the body length mirror for a final time. Looking back at her was a very normal, slightly up-market lady with a now modestly blond head of groomed hair, tastily dressed and whose facial recognition would need close-up study by anyone looking for the escaped prisoner Marguerite Villeneuve. In a couple of days she had changed from appearing to be of low health and haggard and drawn to looking fit and modestly attractive. The last thing she wanted was to stand out from the crowd and draw any form of attention.

She had just set about making the room look truly occupied by leaving clothing and toiletries in their normal places when her bedroom phone buzzed. Her immediate reaction was to run from the room and hide somewhere. But she did not. Some sixth sense, no doubt acquired from years of intensive Parisian training, said very firmly that they could not already be on to her in this place. Her precautions had been total. Gingerly she picked up the phone.

"Jessica?"

"Yes." She knew at once who it was.

"Piet here. Just wondered how things are going?"

"Fine, thanks Piet. So good to hear you. Anyone visited you yet?"

"Yes, but no problem. I knew nothing. Are you any nearer to getting out of the country?"

"Not yet. Working on it. I have to find someone, and after that, another person."

"Maybe I could help?"

"That would be good." Something inside her relaxed. "But how would you do that?"

"A modest meal somewhere this evening? I'm doing nothing else. We can talk about it."

"That would be nice. I'll try to recall how to behave. But we must both be very careful."

"Leave it to me. I know a few good places. I'll pick you up at exactly eight o'clock - it will be dark then and that will protect. Remember where I dropped you off?"

"See you there - and thanks again."

She replaced the phone.

SIXTEEN

Piet arrived bang on time. Jessica was there to meet him. No formalities. Straight in to the car and off.

"A little place I know near here called Joe's Kitchen, now run by a guy called Albert. Good food, few people and friendly surroundings. Each table is private and enclosed. Diners can hardly see each other. It should suit us down to the ground."

"That sounds good, Piet. I am beginning to feel guilty about using up your money so fast. I went off on a shopping binge this morning and it just seemed to evaporate."

Piet cast a quick eye over her clothing. "Blimey, what a difference! That is money really well spent. Incidentally I realised you need a bit more help, the equivalent in cash of one krugerrand if you could use it. I guess that should help get you free of all this and back into France or wherever you are trying to go. Strangely, I really do have a conscience - we were all in it together but on different sides. I don't think my friends in London would agree with me, that's why I have told them nothing. Feel in the side door pocket and take what is there. Some rand, some pounds and the rest dollars."

Jessica felt down and slowly lifted up a wadge of notes. She pushed them deeply into her pocket. Despite the disciplining hardness, sometimes bitterness, that had gone into forming her character from a young age, she was truly overwhelmed at this generosity, so badly needed right now.

"Piet, I am *so* grateful. You've no idea---"

"Yes I have. I saw it all." Piet put his finger to his lips, then changed gear and came slowly to a halt. "Here we are."

Jessica saw just a few people inside the small restaurant as she alighted. They were met by a smiling Albert who showed them to their nicely secluded table around which were comfortable bench-like seats. They sat down and Piet, seeing her for the first time away from the outside darkness, now saw a woman of considerable beauty. The ravages of prison had been removed at his place but whatever had happened since had altered her completely. He was truly stunned. It was all he could do to keep it casual. "You've changed a bit since I last saw you. Almost now unrecognisable, I would say."

"Thanks. Yes, I think they will be looking for a rather different woman."

Albert returned and waited while they ordered. He went off with a smile, white teeth gleaming from a shining black face. These would be substantial meals. His regular customer had found himself a real corker of a girlfriend!

"You know you really have put yourself in danger by helping me. Saving my life might just mean losing your freedom. I would not wish those experiences on to my worst enemy." The full extent of Piet's vulnerability was grinding away at Jessica.

"I realise that! My reaction to seeing you in that awful state in prison has put me right in the firing line. So I'm equally keen to get you out of this country. You do have a husband - a Lord, of all things! I followed you home to check things out long ago."

"Yes, I know."

"You knew?"

She smiled. "Put it down to my training in the Securite Interieur. We were taught how to be aware of most things like that! Yes, I do have a husband. And yet do I? The marriage has never been consummated. It just wasn't like that."

"What?" Piet, looking at such a beautiful woman, could not believe what he was hearing.

"He was sort of homosexual looking for a dolly bird to parade around. What he did not know was that I needed access through him to a variety of influential Brits. I was married to an idea. It worked for us both. No attempt was made by him to contact me in prison. Not surprising, I suppose, when he realised what I had been up to. Probably desperate to keep away from the situation."

"So where are you aiming to go?"

Just then the wine arrived followed by the roast beef meal they had ordered. She held her reply until the waiter had departed.

"I'm Jessica, not Marguerite, and *certainly* not Lady Banforth. I hope there is a passport held near here for me which I can collect and use to get back to the UK. But I have to return via Walvis Bay."

"Passport? Here?"

"Yes, I'm hoping a guy from our organisation is still a free man and has kept all the old administrative matter. The boss, Haffenbacker, lived in Geneva but much of the necessary administration, included passports, was done from here."

"You mean a forged passport in your new name?"

"Yes. They had a range of them in case they were ever needed in a hurry." Jessica looked embarrassed.

"And you know the guy?"

"I have a phone number."

"And Walvis Bay?"

"Well, actually, I wanted to talk to you about that."

"This is getting really intriguing. I'm listening." Piet helped himself to more mustard.

"It is long and complicated. You know when we met in prison I said that I would pay you back. Well it may be that this is the way."

Piet was now completely out of his depth. The business of springing this woman from jail was beginning to look simple when compared to what now seemed to be unravelling. He became wary.

"Let's deal with part one first. You haven't yet phoned that number. Is it written down? Did you hang on to it over the last year? Or do you still have to look it up?"

"None of those. It is in my head."

"It stayed there all the time you were banged up?"

"Yes."

"So you want to get a passport in your Jessica name, then go to Walvis Bay to do something and then continue on back to the UK?"

"Yes." She ate calmly, wondering if it was possible to put the story to him in a way that would not alienate.

"Any chance of my knowing what goes on in Walvis?"

"I'll tell you. You may not be interested. On the other hand it could help you and your friends recover the fortune we have all lost."

"Jessica, we will not again get involved in any bloody skulduggery. We four certainly have had enough of life dodging various damned authorities. We run a small but prospering company and never again will we depart from that." His eyes did a quick furtive look around the room. "But tell me anyway."

"It is nothing underhand, devious or criminal. If it were I would not suggest it or, indeed, get involved myself. You must realise that I have truly learned my lesson in a mighty big way. It really is quite simple. We have to find Adolf Hitler's lost amulet."

"I beg your pardon!!"

"Yes that is it. If I have any success in Walvis Bay maybe I could let you know later. If I fail - well then nothing is lost."

Piet finished his meal and sat back to study the woman opposite him. She was beautiful and intelligent, and yet she had to be bloody mad. What she had just revealed was crazy. He smiled at her.

"You know you really are a Marguerite, not a Jessica!"

She pulled a face at him. "Not in this country, I'm afraid. Nor in the UK. Just in France."

"We haven't ordered a sweet." Piet looked at her enquiringly.

"Just a coffee please. You posh men of the world do your business over the coffee. Make mine a simple americano."

As the evening had worn on the whole atmosphere had mellowed. People were laughing and joking. Wine was flowing and confidences were being exchanged. Jessica had not experienced this sort of thing since her young Paris days. Sleuthing work for France had led on to her being attracted away from her own country and into Breck's Daggers organisation. There had never been much relaxation time. And now arriving was a brandy with her coffee. She took it all in almost pinching herself to be sure it was true.

"So, Walvis Bay?"

Yes, there is a man living there who I think must hold the key to finding the amulet. It would have been hunted for by new Nazis if and when they rose up again. Either they have not or they do not know where to look."

"And you do?"

"Well that is where I cannot be certain."

"Any particular person you are looking for?"

"The name is Karl Winkler."

SEVENTEEN

Alex Fung and his wife Sonya arrived right on time. Elizabeth and I were ready as Jonny guided them in to my office. Giles followed on smartly with the coffee.

"Welcome Alex and Sonya." I pointed to their seats and introduced the other two.

"Good to be here. Not a good climate though. It is raining *again* outside." Alex was up with British weather. We all laughed.

Elizabeth gave us the detail about her recent talks with them. Their experiences of work in Singapore had a remarkable parallel to what Piet did for us in Africa. The size of their previous Chinese employers bore no resemblance to our small set-up, but the actual work they undertook did. The more we spoke the greater was our realisation Elizabeth was absolutely right and that they would be pretty near perfect for the job. Alex would carry out the marketing side, the visits and reports, but Sonya would be in charge of handling the paperwork. That was how they had always worked.

After an hour of discussion I had concluded that these two were certainly right for us. We finished up by agreeing that the job was theirs subject to satisfactory findings by Giles and confirmation about remuneration which had already been discussed with Elizabeth. I suggested they start in about a month's time, but first they were to spend a while in discussions with Piet who should be visiting us soon. Talking with him would complete the picture of the work which we undertook and how he went about it.

When they had gone out with Giles I called Walt of Global to confirm that we could accommodate his plans for Singapore and could go live in about a month. He was delighted and we agreed to meet again the following morning.

EIGHTEEN

Jessica found her man. He answered her call. She used the words they had all had burned into in their minds -
"the leaves are falling from the trees"
- and she was immediately accepted. Jonas arranged to meet her at a spot within walking distance of her hotel. He brought her the "Jessica" passport which, with others, he had kept safely hidden in his house. Then shot off as soon as it was handed over. No greetings. No questions. No other discussion. The situation was too dangerous for them both.

She had told Piet that she would arrange her flights to Walvis Bay and then on to the UK. He surprised her by agreeing with her suggestion that they meet up in London when she arrived there as he was shortly visiting his company headquarters. He said she would need a little more cash before she had settled down somewhere and gave her the name of the small hotel where he would be staying. She had feared he would be pleased to see the end of her, but things seemed to be not quite like that.

Jessica, now desperate to be out of the country of her imprisonment, booked on to a Walvis Bay flight leaving the following morning.

After their evening out Piet had driven his way slowly back to the flat. He had felt surprisingly at home with Jessica. The woman he had planned to marry three years ago had walked out on him. Just like that! It had made him very wary of the female sex ever since. Maybe it was because Jessica actually needed him, not just for getting her freedom, but for guidance thereafter. She was obviously pretty resourceful but he had rescued her from true horror and probably death itself. Nevertheless he had surprised himself by suddenly confirming with her that they meet up again. She may have been pretty nasty to his colleagues but she wanted somehow to make up. Difficult for the others but not such a problem with him.

Dammit he liked her! Very much. But, certainly for now, he had better keep those feelings well under wraps. He would fix the plane to London tomorrow and inform David of his time of arrival. And with luck he would meet up with her again. How his friends would all react was in the lap of the gods.

NINETEEN

The plane for Walvis Bay departed from Johannesburg's O. R. Tambo airport the following day at twenty minutes past ten. Jessica made absolutely sure she was on it. She moved carefully through the departure lounge, looking slowly to left and right. Showing her passport had been very scary, but happily there was no reaction to it but a simple nod.

The uneventful journey to Walvis took just over two hours. She sat quietly, frequently looking out through the window and trying hard to relax. On arrival she moved quickly through the airport and took a taxi to the hotel where she had booked in for one night. Once in her room she put down her one luggage bag and did a small jig around the bed. She was still free and in another country. But then, true to form, her mind switched back to the things she had been trained to do. Not espionage this time, but detection.

Karl Winkler must be found.

At the hotel Reception they were a little helpful. They did not know the name but were able to direct her to a meeting place that was used often by the German speaking community. She followed their directions, walking quickly, and soon found herself looking at a small nondescript building. She moved cautiously through the revolving door entrance. There was nobody inside. She followed through to the kitchen and found herself looking at a man who could be a cook. He was busy cleaning the whole area.

"I wonder if you could help me please?"

He stood up straight and studied her. "Of course. What can I do for you?"

"I am looking for Karl Winkler." She tried to sound as if he was an everyday acquaintance. "I am in a bit of a hurry as my plane leaves later today."

"Yes, no problem." He glanced at the large clock high up on the wall. "I guess he will be in his house right now. Do you know it?"

"No, afraid not."

Come with me."

They went outside and he pointed to a distant side road. "Straight down there. Go right. First house on the corner. The small one. Just tell him Franz sent you. "

Jessica thanked him and walked the five hundred yards or so, thinking and planning all the way. She had to be very careful now. This was the whole reason for the visit to Walvis Bay. The house was old but in a good condition. She pushed at the gate and followed the path which led through a small well-kept garden and on to the front door. She pressed the bell push, crossed her fingers and waited. After a short time a rather bent, elderly man opened up. He was casually dressed and had a sparkle in his eye. He looked questioningly at her.

"Good afternoon. Would you be Karl Winkler?"

"Yes?"

"My name is Jessica Rees-Morgan. I am very pleased I found you. I work with a man who had some dealings with your father many years ago."

That was the first lie.

The reaction was instant. "Come in my dear. That sounds very interesting. You must tell me all about it."

He led her slowly in to a comfortable, rather untidy, lounge and they both sat down. There were about a dozen pictures hung around the walls. One black and white framed photograph grabbed her instant attention. Everything about it looked German.

He caught her eye. "That is Fritz Joubert Duquesne in the centre of the picture. He visited here before the last world war. The local resident Germans thought a lot of him at the time." He waited a short time for her reaction but there wasn't one. "So what can I do for you? Who was it who knew father?"

"Name of Haffenbacker. The acquaintance was short and post war but your father told him he would finish up in this part of the world." The second lie. "We had to research a lot to find you. Very different surname?"

"Yes, my father in later life was still proud of his Nazi connections but did not want me associated with that. Hence the name change from Schneider to Winkler. But that's distant history now. It was a long time ago."

There was a short silence.

Now was the time to put her beliefs to the test. Haffenbacker had said not enough research had been done. She was jumping to conclusions. During his Stasi time he had come across some notes which must have been filed away by one of his thug-like predecessors long before. They had somehow got sidetracked and simply filed the details of what he believed, and now saw, was the key to Hitler's amulet hiding place. There were some very strange symbols written down which Haffenbacker found difficult to understand. He memorised almost everything that had been on that note, then destroyed it.

Years later, using his photographic memory, he reproduced it and showed her. She gave more credence than he to the strange words in English which had been scrawled across the bottom of the small page. In her view this was the clue to finding out more. Right now she was on the cusp. She gave Karl a very straight look and uttered those words.

"The evil that men do lives after them."

She watched him carefully. He was instantly stunned. His eyes seemed to swivel around very quickly. He stood up, then sat back down. Then up again to wander around the room, hands in pockets and a deep contemplative mood. He looked closely at her and out came the response.

"The good is oft interred with their bones!"

Then he grunted. "But you are too young!"

She played along.

"Age is no barrier."

He sat down.

"You have come for it? After all these years."

"Yes."

"Father instructed me very firmly on the day of his death to hand it over without question if ever I heard those words. He learned them somehow whilst he was held in England."

"That is why I am here."

Her heart was in her mouth.

"I promised faithfully to carry out his wishes."

"Of course."

"But you do not look like a Nazi sympathiser."

"Still waters run deep. Things are not quite the same these days." She thought quickly. "The cause has to change with events."

Kurt cleared his throat. "Wait there. I have to find what you want. I have never opened it myself - those were father's wishes."

"Right. Thank you."

He went off and Jessica heard him steadily climbing the stairs. She looked around the room, studying the place in an effort to keep herself calm. Maybe she had hit the jackpot. But equally it was possible that he could be calling the police.

A few minutes later he came back down holding a small package which he carefully handed over.

"It has been locked in the third drawer down inside my bedroom cupboard since the day father died. My duty is now done." He sank back down in to his chair, looking as if a great burden had been lifted from him.

Jessica held the package awkwardly, trying hard not to show how nervous she felt. Her mind had processed this scenario on many sleepless nights in that awful prison. Would she open it in his presence? He would probably expect that, but, more importantly, the package might throw up further questions to which Karl might just know the answer.

"Would you like to see what's inside?" She gave him a friendly we're in this together look.

"Well er yes. It would be most interesting. I have always kept clear of father's politics but just what I have been guarding for him all these years would be good to see."

She inserted her thumb into a gap in the wrapping paper and ripped it open. Inside was a small thin cardboard box from which she removed the lid. There lay a rolled up sheet of paper. She carefully opened it and was instantly disappointed. Written there was a series of symbols which looked very similar to those drawn from memory by Haffenbacker. It looked like a replica of what had been deposited with the Stasi all those years ago. She held it out for him to see.

He studied the detail. In small lettering across the bottom of the page were the Shakespeare words she had given him and to which he had responded. They were what his father had drummed in to him all those years ago. The letter K stood out prominently. There was a cross, a triangle, an arrow and a sort of pendant on a chain with H H written alongside. Two lines went down each side of the page with a circle on top of each and the Shakespeare quotation scrawled across the bottom.

"Looks pretty meaningless to me. What on earth could it be? Father was no fool."

Jessica knew it was the pendant shape which had excited Haffenbacker as he had learned through other Stasi documents of the existence of the amulet. All their sources had said it was missing, whereabouts unknown. Her main objective now was to establish where Karl's father had gone when the bunker was falling.

"I have no idea. Looks like a bit of picture drawing."

"But father said it was extremely important."

"Where was he sent when they picked him up not long before the end of the war, I think?" She made it sound casual.

"Oh, he was held by the British and taken to England for questioning. He was always quite proud of that. It made him feel important I think."

She became icily casual. It really was crunch time. The K meaning was what she had come for.

"Any idea where in England?"

"Place called Kanley, or something like that, was the town where they took him. They flew him over. But nothing much happened as the war ended soon afterwards and a few months later he was returned to what was a very different, and now hostile, Germany."

Jessica made a strong mental note of the name and went on discussing more mundane things with him. He was particularly keen to assure her that, although he associated today closely with the German community, they were in no way Nazi sympathisers. Not these days anyway. And would she let him know if the strange information he had given her ever led anywhere. Any information at all would be very interesting to have.

Her third lie was to nod positively.

Before long she felt it was time to go. She talked about a few pleasant things to avoid being too abrupt and then thanked him profusely for his help, shook hands and left.

TWENTY

The meeting with Global went well.

Walt had called in a couple of fellow directors who also welcomed the new arrangements in Singapore. The idea of a specialist in the area who was not on their payroll but whose expertise was immediately available to them was very attractive.

"If it goes as well in the Far East as it does with your man in Jo'burg the results should be tremendous." Mike Donnat, their top accountant, was very aware of the results we had obtained over the past year for their products in Africa.

"Yes, I've just heard from him. Piet Geldenhuys will be over on a short visit in a couple of days. He usually attends a Board meeting with us every three months or so."

"Get him to call in if he has time. I'd like to have a chat." Walt gave me a quick, slightly agitated, look. "If that's ok with you that is."

"Of course. Absolutely no problem. I'll fix it, Walt."

At exactly ten o'clock the coffee arrived. The mood changed to suit the event. Steven Blatt wanted to know how my wife fitted in to our small operation. "Young children often make it difficult." He had his own problems in this direction as his wife was a high powered teacher and was champing at the bit to be mother and teacher both at the same time.

"Not easy Steve. Most work is done from home in Brighton. I don't have any real answers."

Walt then gave me a folder. He smiled. "Some home reading for you. We have a range of ideas for your consideration. Several new products, some existing ones. All to be introduced to the Far Eastern markets over the next year. I would welcome your views on the order you would consider we should take and the speed your new man can digest the detail and work on it."

I looked slowly around.

They were all unusually keen to start this thing moving and our research was vital to getting the whole thing right. Their faith in us was palpable. I kept my cool.

"I'll go through it all myself and then work with Alex before he leaves for Singapore next month."

Quick coffee finished. We were all keen to get on. We stood up, shook hands all round, and I departed with a spring in my step. We could cope with this and Alex was definitely the man for the job.

TWENTY-ONE

At eleven o'clock the following morning Jessica arrived back to a very autumnal-looking London. She passed uneventfully through Customs, collected her bag, purchased a map of southern England from the airport bookshop, and then made for the Gatwick Express train which would take her to Central London. The long plane flight from Walvis Bay had given her plenty of time to think meticulously through her next movements.

Piet had been extremely generous. His objective was to get her back to London safely where she could then sort herself out. Without his help and kindness she was now sure she could not have survived, indeed would not have wanted to go on at all. She hoped to see him again.

This train went straight through to Victoria Station and was fast. She consulted the map. It was about sixty-five miles from central London to the manor house just outside Cambridge where she had resided with her "husband" Lord Banforth. She knew she must arrive there after dark and avoid being seen. The small village was about the only place in the UK where she might be recognised, despite her changed looks. That could end in complete disaster as the law might well be brought in. Finishing up back in a South African prison with an extended sentence would spell the end for her. It was simply not an option.

In Victoria she went speedily around the shopping areas. She purchased a torch and a canvas bag. What she could not find anywhere was something small with which to dig. It was, unfortunately, not summer-bucket-and-spade-for-the-beach time. Then she spied a small shovel hanging on the wall in a flower seller's shop. It was used by the staff there for potting plants but was just what she wanted. Twenty pounds secured a product worth perhaps five. The final item, which took longer to arrange and purchase, was a mobile phone. Just across the way from the station she had seen a Holiday Inn. She made for it and booked in. There was time for some short relaxation.

After an hour's rest she set about the disguise, having brought all the necessaries with her. Within another hour she had become an elderly woman and was more or less, yet again, unrecognisable. Then she spread out her few belongings in the cupboard and around the room before carefully checking that the spade, torch, mobile and raincoat were in the newly purchased bag. The room key was in her pocket. The phone told her that it was already past five o'clock.

Nobody even glanced at her as she sped from the hotel as quickly as an old woman can without attracting attention and hailed a taxi to take her to King's Cross station. It was rush hour but she still was able to board the train there at just after six. It would be nearly dark on her arrival in Cambridge.

They reached their destination uneventfully. Nothing much about the station had changed in the couple of years she had been away. She hobbled off the train, trying hard to avoid the pushing and shoving of those keen to get home after a long day at work. The queue for taxis was not long and she soon boarded one. She gave the driver the name of the local pub which was a ten minute walk from the manor house. They arrived at the Horse and Hounds after complete darkness had fallen. She paid him and fed her phone with his telephone number so that she could call him for the return trip.

There was laughter coming from the bar. A couple of cars sped past. Now unseen she moved quickly, walking about a mile up the road. There she turned right into the small lane which led up to the manor. She knew the way well and within minutes she had arrived, not at the main entrance gates, but at a place in the surrounding hedge which used to allow access to the grounds for those who knew about it. She shone the torch carefully to find the exact spot, placed her bag carefully on top of the bank, pulled herself up and clambered over, carefully dropping the torch back into the bag. She stood still for a few minutes listening intently. There was nobody around and, happily, she knew that His Lordship hated dogs. She grabbed the bag and moved stealthily in the direction of the manor house.

Although it was dark she could just make out and be guided by the tree branches as they stretched skywards. After a few minutes she came upon a huge oak tree which she knew well. It looked just the same as she had always known it despite her prolonged absence. That was not surprising as it was over a hundred years old. From then on it was simply a question of moving from one tree to another - she had made sure that she knew them all well - until she came upon a modest sized beech. This was it. She had arrived and lowered her bag carefully to the ground.

Again she listened intently to the noises of the night. There was nothing untoward anywhere.

At the tree's base she knew there was a small hollow and felt for it just to confirm, after which she felt in the bag for the spade. From that tree hollow point she measured six of her own foot lengths back in the direction from which she had come and then pushed the spade gently in to the soft ground. Carefully putting her body between the manor house and the marker spade she flashed the torch across the ground immediately beneath her. It may have been her imagination but the grass there did seem slightly thinner. When she had last been in this spot she had left an almost bare patch with loose grass on top to cover up. She extinguished the torch and carefully dug away the surface turf and put it to one side. Nothing happened for a while but then she uttered a sigh of relief when about six inches down the spade hit metal. Her box had been put there in a hurry. It did not take long to pull it out and she held it for a second, earth and all, against her heart. But now was not the right time for any form of rejoicing and she returned to the job in hand.

She had just levelled out the soil and was pushing back the turf when she heard a door bang. She swung quickly around to look at the distant house but could see nothing. It could well be the Estates Manager doing his evening rounds if the system worked as it used to.

Jessica was in no mind to find out. Spade, mud-covered box and torch went quickly into the bag and she returned carefully but quickly the way she had come. She must get away with all speed. The project would only be successfully completed when she had left the area. As soon as she was on the main road she called up the taxi driver. He was just delivering someone to their home but said he would collect her in fifteen minutes time from the Horse and Hounds.

Half an hour later she was relaxing on a London bound train, bag safely held on the seat beside her.

TWENTY-TWO

Three days after my meeting with Global I received a call from Piet who had arrived overnight and was at his hotel.

"Sorry, Dave, I'm a bit later than we had arranged. Something came up."

It was typical Piet, but maybe it was his unpredictability which made him so good at his job.

"I hope the plane journey was easy. Walt at Global would like a chat sometime. Nothing in particular, it seems they just like your work!"

"Yep, good to be appreciated by at least someone! All right if I call in on you this morning?"

"Come right over. Staying in the same hotel?"

"Yes, the best one in the whole place. Nothing can beat it in my opinion. Having gardens like this in central London is pretty rare! Quite close to you too. Be over in half an hour."

He arrived in my office twenty minutes later, shook hands, sat down and immediately pulled from his briefcase the usual sheath of papers for me to read. They would contain his ideas for improvements in how we worked in London, ideas for expansion, and thoughts on the way things were going in his African continent parish. He took his directorship of the company very seriously.

"Thanks Piet. Good bedtime reading. How goes it generally?"

"Very well. But I do have one problem though which will take a while to go into. Some other time perhaps?"

Just then Jonny arrived with the coffee which he put down on my desk before embracing Piet. We were not just business associates but close friends after all we had been through together.

"Piet has a problem to discuss. Can we all hear it?"

I smiled as Jonny immediately plonked himself down and was all ears.

Piet responded brightly. "Yes, of course. It involves all four of us originals really although I realise Elizabeth cannot be here." He turned to me. "How is she - and Teddy?"

"Both fine thanks. Now, what's the problem?"

"You are all going to hate me but I'll give it to you straight." He cautiously sipped his coffee and somehow looked us both in the eye at the same time. I wondered what on earth could be coming. His communications from home had been rather erratic recently but that seemed to me not to be serious. Jonny saw the funny side.

"Whoever suggested we did not hate you already after all---" His words came to an abrupt finish when he saw the look on Piet's face.

"I helped Jessica get out of jail. I damned well did!"

"Who's Jessica?" Jonny asked the question but I already knew the answer.

"Lady Banforth to you."

I gave Jonny a keep quiet and listen look. This could be serious.

Piet continued, "It's a long story which I'll keep short. I heard her name on the News programme at home. She was rabble rousing in the female Johannesburg jail. The sort of offence for which you get an extension of time. Out of interest, and after much soul searching, I went to see her."

"You *what*---?" Jonny was immediately up in arms.

"Quiet Jonny. Listen!" I needed to hear it warts and all.

"I just wanted to chat about the past. She was in jail for fifteen years and I found myself keen to hear her side of the story. But what I found when I visited was simply horrendous. She was going mad, surrounded by mothers with screaming kids, a lack of hygiene anywhere, an inability to converse in the local languages and, at times, very high climate temperatures with no way of cooling things down. She said she was dying and I was sure she really meant it."

"She shouldn't have pinched their krugerrands." Jonny was blunt.

"*We* nearly stole them instead. It could have been *us* inside doing a very sizeable stretch. Anyway, to cut a long story short, she said she could get out but needed transport which could spirit her away. It was the only thing missing from her escape plan. Could I manage that? Under the enormous pressure of my own conscience, and during my second visit, I agreed to help her."

"Dammit man, she pulled a gun on Elizabeth and me!" I was one hundred per cent behind Jonny's sentiments. "Where is she now?"

"Probably in this country. She was, for some reason, keen to get back here. But I suspect she will ultimately finish up in France."

"Are the authorities in South Africa on to you?" Jonny looked grim.

"No. Well not yet anyway." Piet thought better than to tell us he had been questioned and had lied through his teeth, simply denying all knowledge.

"How on earth is she surviving? She jumped jail, presumably penniless, and with no normal clothing. No passport. And we know her associates are also in jail. Or did that guy Haffenbacker also get out?"

"I gave her enough cash to enable her to leave the country. She has a passport that had been held for her in Jo'burg somewhere. That is all I know. Believe me she would definitely have passed away if I had not helped her. Those atrocious conditions were bloody indescribable. She was a totally broken woman. And no, Haffenbacker is in high security for twenty years."

"Well, no problem then Piet. Thanks for telling us." Somehow I did not think he had told all but I hoped his traumatic experience was now behind him. Simply the knowledge that that ice-cold woman was at large gave me real shivers.

"Well, there is just one more thing."

Why wasn't I surprised at that?

"Jessica said she wanted to make up for her past awful behaviour towards us. Apparently she may have the lowdown on where to find something extremely valuable that is hidden in the UK. Nothing illegal or anything like that."

"Any idea what?" Jonny did not sound particularly interested.

"Well yes. It is Adolf Hitler's lost amulet."

TWENTY-THREE

Jessica arrived back at the Holiday Inn late that evening, exhausted but excited. She spread a newspaper across the small table and placed the mud-covered box on it. She recalled that it had no locking device, but clearly the top was firmly held in place after being embedded for a whole year in the ground. Eventually she managed to prise it up with the hotel letter opener. She shivered. This moment marked the end of a dreadful, frightening year when she had felt that death was inexorably on the way. She had planned. She had refined the planning. All through those dark, horrible, incarcerated nights. It still seemed incredible that Piet had shown up to enable her complex escape jigsaw to fall into place.

After considerable manipulation the top clicked off and fell on to the paper. She instantly emptied the box. What fell out was twenty thousand pounds, all in fifty pound notes! Followed by her genuine passport that would get her back into France! All intact and now safely in her care. It was very lucky that she had followed her instincts and taken the precaution of saving in this way when she had money and before partaking in the doomed and illegal Haffenbacker krugerrand venture. Anything else that she still held in her bank account, which was considerable, was probably lost for all time.

There was a knock at the door. She shoved the money and passport out of sight back into her bag and then moved across the room and opened up. The meal looked excellent but she felt almost too churned up to eat it.

This money would enable her to return to a life where she could earn a normal sort of living and forget the awful times she had experienced. When the waiter had departed and the door was again locked she put the notes back on the table and stared at them for a long time. They spelt at least some form of security. She could now afford to stay put for a while. Ultimately she might return to France and live out her days down in the south. But first she hoped to fulfil her promise to Piet about "the project." He should soon be in London. She pulled the scrap of paper she had carefully put in her pocket.

It read simply "The Cloisters."

TWENTY - FOUR

Silence reigned. Jonny and I were stunned. Piet, I thought, looked embarrassed.

"That has to be just a bloody joke." Jonny made as if to go.

"She had one more piece of information to obtain and then she reckoned she would have enough detail to start a search. She felt that we had the right sort of make up to do the job. Good of her to think of us really." Piet smiled weakly.

"Well you can count me out. That woman is dangerous, and that's putting it mildly." Jonny spun around quickly and left the room.

"Me too. Do you know she actually put a bullet into the floor of Elizabeth's flat? It was a *huge* threat to us. Comply or else! You have pretty obviously got yourself entangled with this awful woman and her schemes. I suggest you deal with that but do not involve any of us in it."

"You really do not want to see what this is all about?"

"No!"

"But doesn't it sound intriguing? I mean - something that belonged to Hitler?"

"No."

"Not even a look at the project? Or even the woman, whom I assure you is extraordinarily changed after a year in a South African jail?"

"Jail was their fault. It had nothing to do with us."

"But we could just as soon have been there had we ourselves been clever enough to keep that loot. We're not morally superior to them in any way you know."

"Partially but not wholly true. But still No! Are you trying to soften me up on this subject, Piet? I say it again. Simply----NO!"

Piet could by now fully understand that there was no future to be had with us on Jessica's project. He rose, picked up his bag and turned to find his way out. "Maybe I'll pop in here tomorrow and perhaps we can carry on business as normal. Please forget I ever mentioned anything about Jessica. I'll deal with everything myself in my own way. Sorry I ever brought up the subject!"

And with that he was off.

TWENTY-FIVE

I was unable to sleep.

I reached out quietly and picked up the mobile phone which at night I always place on the small table beside the bed. Then I slowly manoeuvred it down beneath the bedclothes. Once there I pushed the small button. Bright light shone. It was only one in the morning. Elizabeth, beside me, was breathing easy. There was no way I was going to wake her up. I very quietly slid the phone back where it belonged.

The visit that day from Piet was supposed to have been routine, or, at least, that is what I had thought. As things had evolved the get together became explosive and nasty. He seemed to have a pretty big problem and we instinctively beat a hasty retreat almost before he had started. Our reaction was totally understandable. I thought Piet very wrong to equate our efforts to find those lost krugerrands to those of Haffenbacker and Lady Banforth, now Jessica, - how that name grated - as we were actually the goodies in the whole scenario. We were carrying out the wishes of a dying South African friend of Piet's. They had then simply hunted us down and grabbed the loot from us. Moral comparison? We were in the right. But it still was not ours - so perhaps we were not quite as high minded as we felt. Certainly we would not have returned anything to the Mint in Pretoria from whom the cache of krugerrands was originally stolen by a disenchanted white senior civil servant who had headed up their Mines ministry. So maybe Jonny and I were a bit harsh on Piet. Dammit, just why had he helped that woman to free herself? I rolled over in a vain attempt to get some sleep, pulling my pillow down and the blankets up a bit. Five minutes later I turned the other way round and repeated the process.

"You've something pretty big on your mind."

Despite my great care she was on to me.

"Not the usual thing either! Come on. Out with it."

"You do not really want to hear."

"Oh yes I do!"

"Ok, so it's Piet."

"I think I should know about anything affecting a fellow director of *our* company!" She was now well and truly awake and, I could tell, waiting impatiently to learn the detail.

"He helped Lady Banforth, now Jessica, to get out of a South African jail."

"Wow! Really! That *is* something. The woman who, together with her Haff, wrecked my lovely flat in Pimlico. Tell me the story. All of it! No omissions and I do not want it abbreviated. We've all night if necessary."

I groaned inwardly. Once she got hold of something like this she was like a dog with a bone. Telling it all to her it took about half an hour. She remained silent while I relayed everything I knew. When I had finished I turned over, determined to sleep, but I quickly realised that that was now not to be.

"So when are you going to see her?" I had omitted the bit about our refusal to have anything to do with the woman.

"Elizabeth, she nearly shot us both."

"Yes but that was then. She has to be harmless now, and Piet seems to have a problem. Not very helpful of you."

"I need to sleep. I've had a busy day. You know we are already half way through the night."

She growled. "Promise me you will reconsider."

"No, I *cannot* do that."

She kicked me hard in the back of my leg. "No promise, no sleep."

In desperation I promised. Well "reconsider" did not mean that I would actually be going ahead and fixing some sort of meeting, did it?"

TWENTY-SIX

Monday morning was cold and wet. The train up from Brighton had been full of commuters who, as usual, were stoically facing the hell of overcrowded carriages, dripping coats and late arrival. I tried manfully to be one of them but found it difficult, although the one saving grace was that I had a seat beside the window and could stare out at the passing misery.

It wasn't just the train that was upsetting. I had spent a difficult weekend trying to play down Elizabeth's strong desire to meet that dreadful woman. Her reaction to Piet's revelations about Jessica was diametrically opposed to the antagonism felt by Jonny and myself. It was just typical. Elizabeth wanted to know more. Precisely why had Piet felt it necessary to break the law and help her to escape? Why was she returning to the UK - and what had that to do with Hitler's missing amulet? Surely the whole thing required *much* further investigation? And Elizabeth would like very much to meet her again, face to face, just to see what then came up.

My whole weekend had been wrecked. What on earth was I to tell Jonny after our joint fierce protestation to Piet? When Elizabeth got a taste for something like this there was no stopping her. And I had to admit to myself that, as a director of the company and the one who had received the maximum abuse and rough handling by Haffenbacker and Jessica, she was actually fully entitled to a big say in how things went in the new situation.

The train eventually pulled in to Victoria Station and I walked in to the office a quarter of an hour later. Jonny was there and greeted me with a nod.

"Good trip up?"

"Definitely not."

"Good weekend then?"

"No!"

He wandered with me in to my office. I hung up my wet coat and lowered the briefcase to the desk. We both sat.

"What is it Dave? Something's really bugging you this lovely Monday morning."

"It's Elizabeth. She bloody well wants to meet Piet's woman and there's no give at all."

"Oh God! That's torn it." Piet knew how single-minded Elizabeth could be. Her persistence had actually stood us in good stead in the past. But then a strange look passed across his face. "But really I suppose there's no *real* reason why not. Could be quite interesting if we forget the worst of the past. After all Haffenbacker is not around. That woman might be quite different now. You know Elizabeth usually knows exactly what she is doing."

"You're beginning to change our jointly firmly held position on this. Are you a man or a mouse?"

"Sorry, Dave, but we have seen her judgement carry us through all sorts of near disasters. I'm just beginning to think she should have her way with this. I suspect she will want to withdraw from it almost at once. But she should see the woman if she wishes. *Mouse* I guess!"

TWENTY-SEVEN

"Cloisters. Good morning."

"Mr Geldenhuys please."

It was early morning and Jessica held her breath, hoping Piet had arrived as he had suggested in their discussions.

"Putting you through."

"Piet Geldenhuys."

"Piet, its Jessica. Remember me? I wasn't sure you had yet arrived."

"How could I forget? Good to hear you Jessica. Yes, I got in yesterday morning. How goes everything?"

"Just fine. I'm booked in near to Victoria station. Something really good has happened about which maybe I can tell you the story at some time. But what I am really concerned about is that amulet thing." Better not to mention the name Hitler on the telephone - even in free and easy UK.

"Yes, well I spoke to the team yesterday. I'm afraid they are a bit antagonistic. That's to put it mildly. You guys really stirred them up. But maybe I can help you a bit. We might get together some time to discuss the whole thing. Have you had breakfast?"

"No."

"Well maybe you'd like to come on over? Or perhaps you would rather not? They do an English breakfast here to die for. Taxi will take about fifteen minutes from there even in rush hour I would think."

There was no holding back on Jessica's part. "Thanks. I'll be there right away."

Piet met her at the hotel entrance with a small hug. He was very pleased to see her again and led her through to the dining room. They joined the short snake of people, each armed with a plate, and selected bacon, hash brown, sausage, tomato, egg and all the other unhealthy components of a solid breakfast, before returning to the table they had selected. Coffee arrived immediately.

"Really good to see you again Jessica. I had thought you might call it a day and go straight back to France. You have things to tell me?"

"Yes. I am now the proud owner of twenty thousand pounds." She went on to relate to him the full detail of her careful visit back to the manor in Cambridge.

"Jolly well done. Great foresight to hide it in that way."

"Well, I was always taught to plan for the worst, so I did. I can return back what you gave me. That help was very good of you. Saved my life. Really!"

"Don't worry about that, you will eventually need even more cash. But at least it takes the immediate pressure off."

Jessica munched her food with great appreciation. She was still celebrating being out of that Johannesburg place!

"You reckoned you might help with the amulet?"

That brought to the fore the dormant part of Piet's memory. "How did things go in Walvis Bay? Did you find the guy?"

"Yes I found him. And he had the detail which he'd held on to for many years as instructed by his father."

"He handed it over to you?"

"Yes, but it needs interpreting. The big thing is that now I at least know the town where the amulet is hidden. However the paperwork I was given needs a lot of thought. It is not a straightforward X marks the spot."

The town name?"

"He said it was Kanley. I have looked up all sorts of places with that name and have concluded it has to be Kenley which was a huge Ministry of Defence airfield in the war. The Germans pronounce the letter K like CAR. His father was apparently flown back to England after they picked him up in Germany."

"So you look around Kenley aerodrome for Hitler's lost amulet deposited somewhere there long ago by the man's father? Sounds real easy, I don't think."

Just then a tinkle sounded from Piet's mobile which was in his shirt pocket. It was David. He put it on speakerphone.

"Morning Dave."

"Hi Piet. Talk about turning full circle. I thought I had better let you know. Elizabeth has done an Elizabeth. She is very keen to meet and have a chat with Jessica if and when that is possible. Goes completely against my feelings of course!"

Piet looked across at Jessica who nodded affirmatively.

"She is here with me. Just recently arrived. She would love a chat. Any idea when?"

"What about them meeting here tomorrow morning?"

She nodded yes.

"Right. We'll see you then, Dave, and thanks."

"Tell Jessica to leave her gun behind!" I thought a joke was in order. I didn't know it then but Piet told me later that Jessica had looked aghast.

"Will do Dave. See you all then." Piet pocketed the phone.

"So! You and Elizabeth! That sounds like a recipe for the sparks to fly."

"I don't think so. I hope we can make sense of the situation. Sometimes women do things differently. Not quite so black or white. She will no doubt want to give me a telling off - which I deserve. But, you never know, she may interpret the amulet situation in a somewhat better way than the male of the species!"

Piet finished his meal, his thoughts turning to the immediate future. "I think that, as two newly arrived people in London, we might do the rounds? Have you anything lined up for today?"

She did, but her plans instantly became totally flexible.

"No, not really. What are you thinking?"

"Well I myself have never seen the Natural History museum, the V and A, inside St Pauls and the Tower. I could go on. There is a huge list. We could do some of it together perhaps?"

"I'd love to but I will have to go back and change."

"We'll go together and I'll wait for you."

They left, took a taxi back to Jessica's hotel and half an hour later were ready to see what London had to offer.

TWENTY-EIGHT

After they had done several rapid visits to the main tourist traps Piet said suddenly, "Time yet to see you home?" He felt that by now he might be dominating her day.

"You really don't have to. I'm a big girl you know. And you have shown me around a lot of London already."

"Oh, is there somewhere else you would like to see?"

"Well I have never been to St James's park although I used to hear a bit about that area from His Lordship. He would often spend time there, frequently with the high and mighty, when up in Town."

It was a warmish afternoon and things with his friends had now gone well, thanks to Elizabeth. Life had been made a smidgen easier. Piet was a single man, Jessica a married woman who wasn't. And the more he saw of her the more he liked.

"Right we'll go there." Piet managed to stop a passing taxi. On arrival Jessica was immediately taken by the attractiveness of the place. They walked across the bridge over the lake. The ducks were, of course, quacking well and held her attention for some time, as did the fountain. In a short while they came to the St James's café.

"Time for tea." Piet's digestive system was suddenly realising they had not had lunch, such had been the fast moving situation earlier. "And I see they do a lunch menu that continues right through the day. I'm having fish and chips. What about you?"

Jessica, too, was starving despite the large breakfast. "I'll join you. My favourite when in England!"

They ate hungrily. The bottle of white which Piet had carefully selected went down well too. Towards the end of the meal he felt it was an appropriate time to talk about where things were going from here on in. She responded by relaying the full detail of her chat in Walvis Bay and all that went on there.

Piet finished his haddock and chips and fell into a pensive mood. There was a long silence as he drained his wine glass and slowly poured himself a refill, at the same time noting she had drunk very little. Jessica was pretty astute. There really had to be something out there. He muttered the words quietly.

"Do you have a picture on you?"

Jessica smiled. "I've copied another one out especially for you." She reached into a pocket and passed across a folded paper sheet which he opened

"Triangle. Below that letter K. Below again is a chain which could be hanging around a neck with a shape attached - presumably the amulet - with HH written alongside. Under that a cross on top of a large rectangle whose long side runs north south and the letters INN at the bottom, with an arrow pointing downwards to a small rectangle which this time goes east-west. Two long lines each side and a tiny *"The evil that men do"* at the bottom.

Mmm, needs much thinking about. It will replace my book at bedtime tonight. You really reckon this bit of paper, dating from wartime, is the pointer to that amulet's whereabouts?"

"As sure as can be. We simply have to solve it. The design work has to be the key to everything."

Piet slowly pulled out his wallet and carefully slid it down behind the notes. "I'll study the puzzle later. At first glance it doesn't make much sense." He gave her a direct look and smiled. "Beautiful woman, sunny day, gorgeous surroundings. We shouldn't be staring at bits of paper."

He was a man she could trust. The whole history of her rescue proved that point beyond the shadow of a doubt. She liked him. But her training still governed her life. Use men. Don't be used by them. She had always shied away from getting close to any one of them. She carefully but firmly guided his thoughts away from the path they seemed to be taking.

"This is very nice but I think I should be off soon. There is a lot to sort out back in the hotel before I go off tomorrow morning for my first meeting with Elizabeth."

Piet got the message. Inwardly he was disappointed. The feelings he had were clearly not to be reciprocated. They could be close friends but that was as far as it seemed to go. He settled the bill and they made their way out to find Jessica a taxi back to her hotel.

TWENTY-NINE

Treading on eggshells was an inadequate description for my feelings when Jessica arrived to meet Elizabeth. I wanted nothing to do with it and Jonny decided the diplomatic solution was to put the two women together alone in Elizabeth's office. We shook hands all round, exchanged a few pleasantries, and the two ladies went quickly off together.

Piet joined us for a normal business discussion, though I have to say things were somewhat disjointed from the start. We were inquisitive. Piet held the answers. Business matters gradually faded into the background. Jonny could not hold back…….

"So what's all this bloody nonsense about Adolf Hitler, Piet?"

"Well, you know, Jessica thinks in this way she can to some extent repay us for her rather awful excesses of the past."

"And get us involved in another situation? Not at all possible in my view."

"It's a harmless one. Find it. Sell to a museum or collector and share out the proceeds." Piet tried rather unsuccessfully to give the impression that this sort of thing was all in a day's work.

"I think you would find there are formalities to be observed with something like that!" I wanted to drop the whole thing straight away and stop wasting good company time. There were more important things to discuss. "Everything could be hogwash thus far. Find it first. Then is the time to establish what, if anything, you have to do officially." I changed the subject. "Your last reports were superb. Global are acting on them. Well done."

"I will arrange to go and see those guys tomorrow if that suits."

"Great. Keep them sweet. They are very important to us."

It was a couple of hours later that Elizabeth burst into my office followed by an excited looking Jessica. Jonny had taken Piet off and I was left to confront them alone.

"David, we *must* do this." Elizabeth sat down and signalled Jessica to do the same. "It is a safe project and could succeed. That would mean making a good amount of cash for us individually or for the company or both. I see no problem and I think we should take Jessica's offer and try to work out where to find the amulet and how exactly to handle the whole situation with her."

I couldn't help it and looked straight at the woman.

"The last time we met you had us at the point of a gun! Now you want to combine with us. How the hell is that supposed to work?"

"Oh David. That's all history and forgotten. Jessica has been describing to me all she has been through and how Piet helped her. A little charity maybe is called for?"

I could hardly believe my ears! And yet I had been warned by my wife's reactions to the situation when at home. I needed reinforcements and buzzed Jonny. He came quickly in, Piet following on behind. They read the situation simply by looking at our faces.

Jessica spoke quietly. "I'm very sorry about all that happened over those krugerrands. I have suffered for it. I apologise for everything although I realise these are just words. For this reason, and also for Piet's incredible help, I wanted to offer something back. Your wife seemed to think this was possible but it seems not to be so?" She looked despairingly at Elizabeth.

"Well I think we should all help. We are a team geared to this sort of thing. We will not be crossing with any officialdom, laws, crook competitors or anything like that. This is a project which requires deep thought and a knowledge of this country. No guarantees about anything, so nothing to lose and everything to gain. And anyway Jessica and I now really get on like a house on fire. It's just you two men who seem intent on spoiling things. We are having our first head banging get together in Hove tomorrow."

She looked disparagingly at Jonny and me. I thought I detected a twitch of the lips from Piet, a sort of half-hidden smirk. And then Jonny let me down completely.

"Well, I'm not really against the idea. It just seemed funny to be working together with the enemy in such a short space of time. But life can sometimes be like that I suppose."

Elizabeth was never one to fail to press home an advantage. "You see, Dave, the team has come alive on this. It just needs a leader. We could not possibly go on without you. It simply would not be right. Join us. We'll do the work. We really do need your blessing."

It was persuasive. Simple really. All I had to do was completely eat my words and be nice to Jessica. I could not really now simply disregard the whole thing. They all just needed my agreement. And I knew life at home could become damned difficult if I spoiled the party.

No backbone.

No guts.

I grudgingly burned all my bridges.

"Ok we'll go ahead but it must not in any way interfere with our normal work here."

Elizabeth and Jessica positively beamed.

THIRTY

The meeting down in Hove went on for the whole of the next day. Jessica arrived at ten o'clock. Teddy had gone to stay with Elizabeth's mother and I had departed hours before on the train to London. It was destined to be quite a get-together as both women were very positive in their ways. Elizabeth had drawn the curtains and projected on to the darkened wall a much larger picture of Jessica's sketch whose details they could now sit back and study.

"Well, we know that K is for Kenley. The triangle above it could be runways, you know how artists talk about the sides coming closer the farther away from you the picture goes. That could well mean Kenley aerodrome." Jessica had worked out that bit long ago.

"Yes, perspective, great. Then below that is a chain with something hanging from it. Almost certainly this depicts the amulet itself." Elizabeth felt sure there could be no other meaning if indeed this whole thing had any authenticity.

"Right, then we come to the letters HH written beside the amulet - does that stand for anything?" Jessica had been defeated by this one from the beginning.

"I've looked it up. Looks like something to do with Hamburg. The average German thinks of Hamburg when he sees those two letters. Or it could just refer to something in the Cologne trade fair. I really think Hamburg."

"But just what would Hamburg have to do with something hidden in the UK?" Jessica was not convinced and spent some time staring at the ceiling. But then she continued, "Let us move on. A cross linked to a rectangle beneath it. Maybe a sweatshirt with a logo on it? Perhaps like the Knights Templar? As a French woman I am sorry to say it but they were burned at the stake in 1314, but nonetheless they still carry on in a very limited way today. A Christian organisation - hence the cross."

Elizabeth frowned. "Too far-fetched. We could come up with a hundred similar organisations where the cross is applicable. Have you any further evidence for this?"

"No, just surfing around really. I agree. We really have no clue on this one."

They sat back, staring at the challenge beaming down from the wall, both aware that so far not much headway had been made. Certainly nothing that really held water. Jessica went on unabashed.

"And two balloons on strings on either side? Well, better news on the INN and the arrow pointing downwards to the small rectangle. INN in imperfect English could convey the message - INNside - and the small rectangle below could be a box. How about that?"

"Well it *could* be Jessica but I'm not sure it actually shows two N's. It could be an M written badly. The whole thing looks more "back of envelope" stuff rather than having been carefully planned. And the wording at the bottom may be Shakespeare but seems to be of little help in our quest and, from what you say, may simply be a sort of password."

Elizabeth went over and drew back the curtains and they sat quietly for some time, each pondering deeply as they mulled over the detail which had been so vividly portrayed.

Now was the right moment to introduce the plan Elizabeth had been hatching for some time. The next move was very clear. "We need to bring in Piet and David, and that means Jonny as well, and really set this up as a serious investigation. Piet went through everything with you in Africa, and David - well he can be extraordinarily bright sometimes - but please do not tell him I said that!" They both giggled. "It is the only way if we are really serious, and I think we are."

"Ye-es. But won't Piet be off back to Pretoria shortly?" Jessica deep down did not want that but realised it was inevitable.

Elizabeth eyed her closely. "You rather like him don't you?"

Jessica remained poker-faced. "Nothing I would admit to."

"That speaks volumes, but your secret is safe with me." She smiled. "Yes, he will be going back and forth but I understand he may be spending some time here talking with our new man who will shortly be on his way to Singapore." She shook her head as if shaking away the cobwebs. "Let's go and have a look at Brighton, find a place for lunch and then follow that with a blow on the pier. Sitting here like two dummies is getting us nowhere in the search for the Fuhrer's necklace!"

THIRTY - ONE

Franz Hoffmann was a person of surprising depths. To the world in general he was a seventy year old married man with adult children who had lived in Walvis Bay seemingly for ever. His wife of forty-five years was of Afrikaner extraction and the two kids grew up speaking a mixture of ungrammatical Dutch, good German and reasonable English. He loved the life and over the years had earned his living taking tourists around in the season, driving a taxi at times and, more permanently, cooking in the local German food restaurant which he now managed. Over the years he had become a feature of the place, dependable if any difficulty arose and reliable in any rare emergency.

His father, Gerhardt, was one of many young Germans who fled to Southern Africa in 1946 after the war. He, like Schneider, whom he had met from time to time, was a fervent Nazi at heart, but, for sheer self-preservation, had hidden his extreme views to all but his son, Franz. Over the years, secretly and willingly the boy was taught and accepted his Aryan creed and all that went with it. He learned too that his beliefs had to lie dormant until the time came.

Gerhardt had settled for a while in Windhoek before finally moving the family to Walvis Bay where he had at last found himself a job which gave him a reasonable living. He forever remained a convinced and ruthless Nazi.

The lady's visit to Franz's German restaurant asking after Karl Winkler was very unusual. In this closed community such things like that rarely happened. It was normal to get more detail. Soon after her visit Franz made sure to spend time with his friend Karl. In the course of a friendly conversation he asked about the woman whom he had directed Karl's house.

Karl, now free of his father's strictures as he had passed on the sealed package, was only too happy to relate all the details, as he knew them, to Franz. They smiled and laughed about it all. How long ago this had all happened and, really, in this day and age, the whole idea of Nazism, with what Franz inwardly sensed from the design description might just be the amulet re-emerging from its slumbers, was rather crazy.

Franz memorised carefully every bit of detail that Karl had related and later returned back to his home deep in thought. To him, with his deeply held beliefs, the information he had might be very important. Possible dynamite, you might say. He would urgently ask to convene a meeting of that very selective breakaway section of the Broederbond-Nazi alliance to which he had always belonged. This was a Southern African organisation so secret that most people had no idea even of its existence. It met rarely. Its members were tough, intelligent believers in all that the Fuhrer had stood for so long ago.

The amulet encapsulated everything.

THIRTY-TWO

It had taken all of two days for Elizabeth to get her way. The old gang plus Jessica assembled at 10am. It was Saturday. Most of London was away relaxing after a busy week and we had the place to ourselves. Elizabeth elected to use my office as it had a largish table around which we could all sit and she then took control of the meeting as we had agreed at home. She had already pinned a large design to the wall.

"This is what we have to study, think about, and eventually solve. It is a plan whose solution will lead us to the hidden amulet which has been deposited somewhere safe since 1945. So safe that nobody has found it. But then it seems unlikely that anyone has even looked. Jessica followed her instincts, went to Walvis Bay, and was proved right. All we have to do is solve the riddle which was set out so long ago to be a guide to the amulet's whereabouts. Does anyone have any problems with this?" She looked menacingly around the room.

There was dead silence.

"Good. David has said he will make notes of everything that comes up. From those notes somewhere could be clues which we can build upon. What do we know so far? Well, not much, but Jessica and I have thrashed out a few initial ideas." She looked directly towards her new-found friend.

"Well yes. Initial thoughts only. Nothing set in concrete except one thing. I am very sure the K shown is for Kenley, famous for its airfield, and we think the triangle at the top may well be the converging lines of the runways there, rather badly drawn. Below that is a representation of the amulet. We're a bit unsure of the rest - and are seriously open to all suggestions!"

I couldn't resist despite being demoted to being Elizabeth's assigned scribe.

"The Shakespeare quotation at the bottom. What's that all about?"

"I do have the answer to that." Jessica gave a winning look all around. "I repeated the words to my contact in Namibia and it immediately opened the door to everything else. It is the password which only he and his deceased father knew had to be used by any convinced Nazi undercover person who was aware of the lost amulet which he must then find. Over the decades it would have become of critical importance to the Nazi cause. I seem to have been the first one to turn up!"

I scribbled it all down in the minutes. Piet had been studying the wall.

"The cross. Could be a church?" He looked across at Elizabeth who responded rather vaguely.

"That, or some sort of Christian organisation. The cross is as wide as it is long, an unusual shape to be seen on a church maybe?"

Jonny had been quietly studying the bottom part of the rectangle. "INN - would that be something significant in German? It was a German who designed the whole thing so very likely to be something in his native tongue. Who speaks any German?"

"We looked it up. An inn in German is Gasthaus - nothing to help there. Maybe it was bad English simply meaning IN?" Jessica didn't seem at all hopeful about this.

Jonny, who had little knowledge of all the history, asked a favour, whilst looking apologetically at the rest of us. "Jessica, I wonder if you could very briefly summarise the background to all this? I feel a bit in the dark."

"Certainly Jonny. Long ago my former colleague, who is now in a high security jail seemingly for life, was a young Stasi officer in East Berlin. He came across an old filed set of notes showing something similar to this design and explaining that this would lead future Nazi leaders to the whereabouts of the amulet. It had been deposited with them by a German communist called Gunter Weber, who had been incarcerated with Schneider by the British, and seems to have been filed and then completely ignored by the Stasi. Years afterwards Haffenbacker made a mental copy of the design and then destroyed everything as the Stasi fell and the Wall came down. At heart he was actually very much a capitalist and felt he might engage in the search one day, in his case the motive being profit. The only other piece of relevant information was that the man who had hidden the amulet in the first place, Adolf's right hand man, was definitely called Abelard Schneider. He shot off to South Africa as convinced Nazis were by then becoming most unpopular in Germany."

So you saw Schneider in Walvis Bay?" Jonny was getting there.

"Not quite. He would have been extremely old. In fact our deepest researches came up with the fact that he had a son, now himself in his seventies, called Winkler. Almost certainly a name change to lose the Schneider image. My guess was that the son would know something. I visited him *and he did!* Quoting

Shakespeare to him opened the floodgates. To Winkler I was the messenger from those who would rise as the new Nazis. He told me of his father and explained that he once was of the faith but no longer. He handed me detail of the whereabouts of the amulet and this more or less matched Haffenbacker's sketch of long ago. He assumed I had the means to follow up on the information and that the Nazis were now possibly on the rise again. I think he himself wanted nothing to do with that and was simply carrying out his father's wishes."

"Thanks Jessica. I've caught up." Jonny smiled at her. "But are there any now around who would also be looking for the amulet. Hitler was a virtual God to them. No way do we want to get involved in another situation!"

"Seventy odd years later. I hardly think so. But you don't have to come on this journey---"

Elizabeth cut in. "We've already decided it is all systems go. I think we all need to study the sketch, each in our own way." And she handed a personal copy she had prepared to each person present. "Study it. Think it through. Come up with ideas, however outlandish. Next meeting one week today. Same time. Same place. Any comments?"

There were none. We disbanded quietly and, dare I suggest it, obediently!

THIRTY-THREE

Piet made it clear that he was now staying on for about a fortnight. He still had to go and see Global as they had requested, and then help to sort out Alex and his Singapore operation. And he was, of course, keen to have an input into the problem Jessica had set us.

I, too, was becoming a little more persuaded that there was something in Jessica's story. Her account certainly had the ring of truth about it. It would be fun trying to find the amulet and maybe remunerative too. Perhaps the approach of winter was a bad time to be contemplating a succession of visits to Kenley airfield - the weather could be pretty inhospitable but that was not really a major problem. I decided to visit there on my own just to have an initial look and get some idea of the layout of the place and the size of the task facing us.

Two days later, in addition to making one or two business calls, I swerved away south to Kenley, arriving at the famous aerodrome in the early afternoon. I parked by the pavement and wandered in through the swing gate and up some steps. It was immediately clear that the whole place had been turned into an RAF war memorial. The original shelters had been re-bricked but the entrance doors to them were locked. There were pictures showing war situations and heroes who had died in the fight. They were permanently positioned around the perimeter road. And adjacent to the entrance in front of a rejuvenated shelter area was the main feature depicting RAF personnel in uniform, all carved in stone.

The whole place was massive. The two runways were still intact. Gliding seemed now to be the only flying activity and there were one or two buildings associated with that. Way over in the distance was the old officers mess. The main airfield was completely fenced off but with access gates which were left open for the public when no flying was in progress.

I decided to walk around the perimeter road which looked to be a distance of about a couple of miles. From our investigation point of view the place seemed incredibly large and complex. Where would we start looking? I passed more shelters, a weather sock flying near to a small weather station, and then some patchy concreted areas now grown over with greenery. There was very little which could possibly relate to the clues we had been given. During the saunter around I saw some dog walkers, a few runners and a couple of loners like myself. But no military personnel were on view despite the whole place being the property of the Ministry of Defence.

It took me over half an hour to complete the walk around the whole airfield. Relating our list of clues to the ground area here threw up an idea or two but really nothing positive. The two crossed runways could, for example, have something to do with the lines shown in that diagram, thus validating what the two women had always reckoned. And I had looked at the historical records of wartime Kenley showing the airfield as it was then. Again nothing much stood out as being related to our investigations. But we were in early days. I took a considerable number of pictures on my phone. They maybe would add something and feed in to the search work we were doing.

On completion of the trip around I descended the steps, exited the gate, and slumped back down in to the car to mull over the situation. There had seemed so little to consider and yet now there was so much. There were buildings, bunkers, small and large concreted areas, a strange looking firing range and many other features, any one of which could hide a tiny amulet. This was not the way. I felt that we must try to solve those clues or we would get nowhere.

THIRTY-FOUR

The meeting was arranged for the last day in November at the farm owned by Adriaan Kloppers which was situated to the north of Cape Town. An urgent call from Franz Hoffman in Walvis Bay was met with instant action by the extreme group of Nazi sympathisers who reacted instantly to the news. They came mainly from their homes in the Free State.

It was cool inside the heavily insulated farm office. Kloppers had rearranged the furniture to enable the eight visitors to sit around a large table. Cool drinks were to hand, but nothing alcoholic. These meetings rarely happened and when they did they were sober affairs.

No minutes were kept.

Information was stored in the mind.

That way no prying journalist, political pundit or even just an ordinary member of the public who would ever penetrate the organisation. For years their existence had remained unknown and they were determined to keep things that way.

In 1973 Eugene Terre'Blanche had founded and led the Afrikaner Weerstandsbeweging or Afrikaner Resistance Movement, known by its abbreviation as AWB. Afrikaner nationalist. Neo-Nazi. White supremacist. He held the position until 2010 when he was murdered on his farm. Steyn von Ronge took over.

It was at that time that several of the most committed "Nazi" members felt the need for something less openly violent and known to the public at large. More secretive. More cerebral and therefore capable of carrying out investigations, atrocities or whatever was called for in the given circumstance, but always remaining beneath anybody's radar. They had carried out assassinations, ruthless torture to obtain information, and theft in furtherance of their ideals. Never once had they been caught as, to the big wide world, this Nazi hierarchy simply did not exist.

These eight visitors had hurried in from their homes and work places. They ran their businesses and farms in the normal way and, although still on friendly terms with old AWB associates, kept their distance. In no way did they wish to be seen in any way to transgress against the ruling democratically elected government of the day as that would ruin their cover.

There were no preliminaries. They started speaking in Afrikaans and then switched automatically to English when Hoffman started showing some lack of fluency.

"We have a report from our member in Walvis Bay. It was so important that I immediately convened this meeting to consider the implications." Aiden Kriel looked around the table at all seven other visitors plus Kloppers and, of course, Franz Hoffman. Their faces already showed intense interest. These meetings were rare occurrences.

"It has come to our notice that the Fuhrer's amulet may have been found. You will know that the whereabouts of this symbol of supremacy has been a mystery to us all since the Second World War. Franz Hoffman, our only member resident in Namibia, has news for us. Franz."

"Thank you Aiden." He nervously cleared his throat. "Well, gentlemen, late last month I directed a rather harassed lady to my friend's house. Her name is

Jessica Rees-Morgan. His is Karl Winkler. I later learned from Karl that he had handed over to her some important details held by him for many years at the request of his father. I feel it is strongly possible they showed the whereabouts of the amulet that all of us and our predecessors have been aware was missing since our leader died in that awful bunker at that dreadful time."

"Wow." Nelius Swart could not hold back. "Revival indeed! That item was not just a piece of jewellery. It had powers. It would bring great renewal to the cause."

"How do we find that woman?" Hansie Steenkamp was less excitable, more down to earth.

"She went to London."

"Big place. Any more detail?" Steenkamp could feel this job coming his way.

"No nothing. Except that she came from Johannesburg where we think she lived. So a London hotel would be likely to be her residence for a time unless she is staying with friends. I have managed to obtain her plane details but that is all." Franz pushed the paperwork across the table to Steenkamp.

"Not much to go by. What about personal details?"

"She was attractive. Late twenties, early thirties I would say. Very much English speaking but maybe a small accent from I know not where. Definitely not Southern Africa. Modestly dressed. She was in a hurry. Told my friend she was off on the plane that same day."

"Not bloody much to go on." Steenkamp needed more. There were growls of agreement from the others around the table as he asked with a rising voice, "Where on earth do we start looking?"

Kriel, the oldest man present and self-appointed chairman of the meeting, tried to keep things in some sort of perspective. They really must not fail to investigate this matter fully.

"Her full name is known. Details of her flight to London are in our hands. We know roughly her age, her looks, and her style of speech. Hansie, given the funding, have you with your contacts in the UK the ability to follow up as quickly as possible - the usual sort of thing - taxis, hotels, maybe the internet? We really have to move fast on this one."

"No problem. I can be in London two days from now. In the meantime I can start things off there immediately. The usual coded emails. I will relay all findings to you, Aiden, and you will no doubt keep everyone informed. But we still have very little to go on." He looked sharply at Hoffman.

"There is a bit more I can relate which might somehow help. My friend Karl told me that she gave him the key words, which he had waited half a lifetime to hear, that immediately gained his total confidence in her as the right person. They were ---*The evil that men do lives after them.* Just why his father used those words goodness knows."

"It's Shakespeare and his father was held in England." Kloppers had studied the Bard long ago.

"There's a bit more. The place where the amulet was hidden he told me had a name something like Kanley. That really is everything I know."

Aiden Kriel realised they were not going to get any more useful information and nodded towards Steenkamp.

"Well Hansie. All systems Go. Any funds you need will be available. Call us for help. We must follow this up and *find the woman*. That seems to be the only way to progress the whole matter. Where is she? What is she up to? Who are her accomplices? To what lengths do we have to go to get that jewel?"

"I accept the challenge and will take two colleagues. I will achieve. God help me!" Hansie smiled as applause erupted all around.

"Lunch in the farmhouse." Kloppers studied his watch."All prepared and waiting. Business complete?"

Kriel told Steenkamp that the barest of detail would be on his mobile phone. No other record of the meeting would be kept. They stood and quietly and reverently muttered the words "Heil Hitler". It sounded almost like a prayer.

Aiden Kriel then declared the meeting closed.

THIRTY-FIVE

The next Elizabeth meeting took place one week later as planned. Another Saturday. Another day not spent with my son in Hove. My office of course. Elizabeth and I had agreed item one at home and out it came.

"Jessica, this investigation may take some time. We would like you to stay in my old apartment in Pimlico which we only occasionally use. It is near here and will save you a fortune in hotel bills."

"Really. That would be wonderful. But surely you need it at times?"

"No, very ok for you to have for the next few weeks I suggest you move in tomorrow. We'll go over later today and I will show you around and give you the keys."

That was that.

"Now, item two. David's visit to what we will call the target." She looked hopefully at me. I hadn't much to say to the meeting that was in any way positive.

"Kenley is what I would call a normal airfield. Two runways, wide open spaces, war-time bunkers, firing range, and the whole place these days used for flying gliders only. Relating all that to the clues we have is tricky. I would say near impossible. One thing I know for sure is that we cannot thoroughly search the huge airfield. Is the amulet buried somewhere under acres of tarmac? Or in the many more acres of grassed areas? Could it be in one of the huge bunkers deep inside a brick wall? If we cannot get the diagram to tell us something we are almost certainly lost. That has to be the only way."

There was total silence all around. The death wish already? They knew I was sceptical about the whole thing. Then, quite suddenly, Jonny came alive.

"I do not think the lines at the top are a converging runway. I think it is a triangle and very roughly represents England. See how the left line is a sort of hypotenuse to the other two lines. And they do not actually meet at the top. Scotland is up there? Look at any map of the United Kingdom, ignore rugged coastlines, and you have that triangle. Together with the K beneath the clue starts to read quite sensibly - England, Kenley."

"Of course! I think that's right! The beginning of the address. Great thinking Jonny." Piet felt for once they had something. Still tenuous. But something.

"Moving on. We pretty certainly know that the chain and what hangs on it is the amulet. Has to be or this whole exercise is null and void!" Elizabeth looked around expectantly. "So then what is H H? We came up with all sorts, often leading to Hamburg. I can't think that the Hanseatic City of Hamburg has much to do with what we are about. German, yes, but there seems to be no other connection to our problem."

There was another prolonged silence. Coffee cups were drained and brains strained over the two letters. For a while they could all sense the massive brain searching efforts that were taking place. But this time no bright spark suggested anything and we soon relaxed into chatting about what wartime Britain was like, and particularly the Kenley aerodrome.

Only Piet did not join in, his mind still wrestling with those two letters. He was on to something which even he knew was not right but could be going a sensible way. He shouted out at Jonny, drowning all casual conversation.

"What about His Holiness?"

"Surely that's damned rubbish. We're not talking Popes!"

"OK, Her Holiness then."

"Piet where does that fit in?" Elizabeth tried cooling things. There followed an awkward, almost embarrassed, silence.

Then out it came.

"I *know* what it is." Jessica said it gently but firmly.

"What then?" Piet stared at her.

"Your comments got me there Piet. Just what do two aitches stand for?"

"Well what?" Three of us spoke in unison.

"It's obvious!"

"What?"

"Heil Hitler! Don't you see? A confirmed Nazi simply confirming his unshakeable beliefs. Stuck in the awful UK, a prisoner, but with an enormous secret. The Nazi certainties would be sure to rise again and he held the key. By writing H H he was shouting revival from the hilltops and the impetus for that was contained in this trinket."

I knew she was right. We all instantly knew that. One of those things. When you have the answer the question looks simple and you wonder just why it took so long.

Two hours went by. We got no farther and broke up. Elizabeth drove Jessica to see her new temporary home and then returned to pick me up for the journey down to Hove. Jonny went quickly back to his place and Piet strolled to his hotel. We had all vowed to put our minds to the remaining symbols and come up with answers in time for the next meeting.

THIRTY-SIX

Sunday afternoon.

The day after their meeting.

Piet was kicking his heels. The weather was, well, British early winter. The lack of sunshine was getting to him. He had spent the morning in the hotel trying to solve something more of the amulet puzzle. But without any success. He was beginning to accept most of the reservations on the subject. But he wanted to support Jessica having been with her from the beginning.

Jessica!

He wondered how things were going with the Pimlico flat. He had the phone number which he had acquired during previous visits. Was she busy? Available for a chat? Or should he keep clear? It took him all of a minute to risk a call. After half a dozen rings she answered.

"Hello."

"Hi Jessica. Piet here. Just wondered if you were settled in yet?"

"Yes, Piet, just finished. I was going for a walk but it is pretty miserable outside. I'm having to get used to the British climate again."

"Yep, I know. I spent nearly the whole morning trying to puzzle out you know what. I failed miserably."

"So you're just kicking your heels right now?"

"Well--yes."

"Come round to tea if you like. I owe you a bit of hospitality."

"Love to. I know where you are. Been there before."

"See you in half an hour or so?"

"Thanks Jessica, I'm on my way."

Piet returned the phone to his pocket, collected his coat and made his way down to the car park. He was one happy man.

At least she hadn't shut him out altogether. On arrival he found a parking place. The door was partially open. Her voice flowed out.

"Hello Piet. Come in and make yourself at home. It really is getting chilly."

He looked around. Not much had changed. On closing the door he was pleased to see that although it had long ago been bashed down by Haffenbacker accompanied by Jessica, it had been well repaired. Ironic that she should be living here after all that unfortunate history.

"Come over and have a comfortable seat Piet. Tea coming up shortly."

He left his coat by the door, moved over and sat down.

"Are you *any* further along the discovery road? I've been at it flat out all morning and haven't really got anywhere."

She called out, "Me too. I try to think as I go along. But nothing seems to mean anything. We will get there of course. Elizabeth said so!" Jessica then reappeared from the small kitchen with a tray of tea with cakes. She sat down and poured.

"I was very pleased to hear you. Thought you might have given me up. One can be quite lonely on a day like this."

"Me too. I couldn't have gone on through the afternoon with any more of the puzzling." He looked meaningfully at her. "I promise not to crowd you with the man-woman thing."

She sipped her tea and looked downwards at her cup. "We were always instructed to beware of human friendships, particularly male ones, as they could very easily interfere with the work. I have always stayed rigidly with that."

"Never had a boyfriend before then?"

"No. I stuck to the regulations."

Piet changed the subject. "I've been wondering. Have you many relations in France? And will you ever go back to see them?"

"I want to be absolutely sure I am totally free from all that South African stuff before I do. I think I am, thanks to you, but there can be many a slip. For example, I had a feeling that I was followed here from the hotel. I checked carefully. It was probably nothing but I suspect things more than most people. I have a mother who I contacted the other day. She was frantic. I settled her mind with a pack of lies. I have a brother who works in Toulouse - far too busy with aeroplanes to bother about me.   That's about it. And you? I hear you had a girl friend?"

"Yes." He swallowed cake and drank down the tea while he frantically thought. "She wasn't keen on me and broke it all off."

"I'm so sorry to hear that. These things can be painful."

There was a long silence. This small flat suited Elizabeth while she lived here. Everything was tidily arranged. The furniture fitted in well and the pastel shades of the place were just right. Eventually Jessica removed the tray and crockery to the small kitchen and came back and sat down. They had chatted for another hour or so when Piet felt he had stayed long enough. He rose, collected his coat and turned to say goodbye. She was standing right up close beside him.

"Thanks Jessica. That was marvellous."

Her voice was very quiet. "Perhaps a small thank you hug?"

He put his arms around her staying longer than he should. He kissed her, a simple goodbye kiss of course. She did not pull away.

Then he left.

THIRTY-SEVEN

I could not attend their next get-together. A month ago I had arranged two business meetings in the West Country, one in Bristol and the other in Plymouth. The latter was the most interesting - a manufacturer of boats looking for overseas markets. The Bristol people were, in my opinion, not yet sufficiently geared up for exports, but I was going to check it out anyway.

After an easy drive down the M4 motorway I arrived on time at my Bristol destination. Cradle Carpets had two directors who welcomed me in. But, as I suspected, we got nowhere. They did well on home sales but were, in my opinion, a couple of years off the company being able to finance going global. They actually went along with my assessment and we agreed to meet again at a later date.

Onwards to Plymouth and Streamline Boats. On arrival I slowed down not far from the Barbican and nosed my way in to park in their premises. Several boats nearby were in various stages of construction and I knew their order book was very healthy. A ruddy faced man came out to greet me.

"Stuart Tope. You must be David Johnston?"

I scrambled out of the car and shook his outstretched hand.

"Yes. Correct first time. You look very busy."

He shrugged. "It's all the year round. Many of these are due out for next summer. We are working like the devil to get them finished in time for the season. Come along in, it's cold out here."

We entered his office, an old building which had been partially renovated. The inside looked modern and smart. The walls were covered with pictures of boats they had made, large and small. We sat at his desk.

"These days the more luxurious the boat the more profitable. That is a general rule but a good guide to the business. We do the smaller ones here. Big expensive stuff is made the other side of the city." He nodded in a westerly direction.

"And you are looking at Africa, particularly those huge lakes?"

"Yes. Smaller boats, but high quality. We have heard there are quite large amounts of cash chasing good small boats out there these days. That's the market we are after."

We talked business for an hour or so and then he showed me over the variety of power boats he had in mind. Some designed for fishing, others purely leisure. "Thirty to forty footers. Air conditioned, all the normal temperature controls. Standard navigation. Top quality fitments right through - seating, beds, some with fly bridges. Comfort and convenience in all cases, to include, of course, refrigeration and cooking arrangements."

I took it all in, noting the most salient points. He then gave me detailed designs, sizes, prices and all information necessary to produce the first stage report of how to go about marketing the product. His most telling comment forced me to expand on the information I would be passing on to Piet. "And don't forget engine servicing and boat safety instruction. All of that will have to be handled locally!"

We chatted a while longer. Then I departed, happy to have a really good new client. I found a small, warm restaurant close by. It had become even colder and was now raining quite hard. My watch showed nearly four in the afternoon. I called Elizabeth and told her it was not going to be an easy drive all the way home in the dark. We both agreed a stop somewhere overnight was sensible. I ate my fish meal and enjoyed the coffee afterwards.

There was a place I had always wanted to see. Postbridge, bang in the middle of the moor. Something from my past. Dartmoor had always held a fascination for me. Now was my chance. I settled the bill and collected the Honda from the boatyard, getting pretty wet in the process. I fed in Postbridge details to the car satnav and drove off ready to follow that lady's very positive instructions. It was difficult to see much of Plymouth or to study the surrounding district leading out to Yelverton. The wildness of the moor passed me by as the rain was now even harder and all my concentration was centred on following the road. After a fraught forty-five minutes driving I turned, as instructed, into the smaller B3212 which I knew led directly to Postbridge. This road was becoming more of a track, thanks to the foul weather. My wipers were finding some difficulty in keeping the windscreen clear, so much so that I was just contemplating turning back when I was forced to screech to a halt. The large van, whose top half was coloured green and the bottom red, which had cut in at the turning and whose lights I was thankfully following, suddenly pulled up in front of me and left no way to pass.

I was given the shock of my life as two men jumped out, ran back to my car and ripped open my two front doors. One had a small pistol. For the first time in my life I felt I was being robbed? But I had nothing they might want.

"Out."

I staggered into the awful weather, shaking with shock. What the *hell* was going on?

"In to the truck!"

The gun etched out the direction.

"I'm sure you've made a mistake. I don't think—"

A third man appeared from the front of the van having jumped to the ground. He then got into my car.

"Go over to the van. Now! Hurry!"

As I walked forwards I heard my car rev up and realised it was being driven away well off the road. Maybe they were hiding it! But why?

"In!"

He pushed me inside so sharply that I tripped and fell across the van's floor. He followed and sat on the far side looking at me, gun at the ready. The other man frisked me and took my phone and wallet. He dropped the mobile to the floor, stamped hard, crushed it, and then hurled the pieces out across the wild moor. A flat wooden surface beside the gunman opposite acted as a small table. My wallet was dropped on to it. I rose up unsteadily from the floor, wet and shivering, and then slowly sat facing him.

The driver of my car returned shortly to take up his position in front. He was undoubtedly the permanent driver of the van. We moved slowly off. Unsurprisingly, given the weather, there was no other traffic around. Nobody spoke. I wondered what on earth this was all about, still firmly convinced they had got the wrong man. In about five minutes we pulled off the road, drove across some pretty soggy moorland,

and half a minute after that we stopped. The gun toting thug seemed to be the leader. He did not move but just kept pointing that damned thing at me. It was unnerving to put it mildly.

"I will not beat about the bush." I noted the accent. Not German. Possibly Australian? But no, it was a guttural sort of noise. Then I had it! *South African!* I became really scared, my brain instantly putting two and two together.

"We need to know the whereabouts of the lost Hitler amulet. It is our property. Give me the information and you can go. Failure to do that will lead to much pain and distress for you. We will not leave you alone until we have that detail." He then pushed a button on what I made out to be a miniature recording machine resting beside him.

Being really frightened makes the mind move faster - well, mine anyway - as I became aware of the exquisite horror of my position. They must have somehow have tracked Jessica all the way from Africa to London and checked out where she went. All her movements! From then on our name was in their sights. Mistakenly, they probably reckoned that I, the company boss, knew everything. Somehow they had followed me and arranged this reception party. I hadn't noticed being tailed but then I simply was not looking. All in all they must have put in a massive amount of organisation. I noticed a couple of coils of thin rope beside the man's seat - my restraint perhaps?

The driver stayed put in his seat up front, insulated from the rest of us. Gutteral man's accomplice thumped himself down menacingly beside me. These guys meant business. It was written all over their faces.

My survival was in my hands. I was alone, dreadfully alone, with three monsters.

"Well, where?"

I decided it would be better not to deny any knowledge. It would be the beginning of God knows what if I did. Direct lying and playing for a little time while I tried to think this thing through was best.

"How do I know you will let me go if I tell you?"

"You have my word."

I took that with one enormous pinch of salt.

"If you could possibly put that gun down I can think more clearly. It is very off putting to be looking at a weapon like that. I'm not used to those things."

"Ok. Not a problem." He jacket pocketed the gun, nodding knowingly at his associate.

"Now you can tell us everything." The man beside me spoke.

I mulled that over before replying to them both slowly and carefully.

"Well, yes, as a matter of fact we think we do know where it is. We have only visited the site once as the situation is a little complex. It is in one of two bunkers on an airfield. There is a concrete base in the construction and the amulet is encased in the concrete just inside the entrance to one or the other. The amulet is low down on the left hand side. Not a big deal to us. Is the amulet of some value to you? Do you have any Nazi association?"

"Never mind that!" He snapped back ferociously at me. "Which airfield?"

I watched the face opposite very closely as I hissed out the answer slowly.

"Kenley."

Satisfaction.

He already knew.

Such information I realised could only have come all the way from Walvis Bay! My face registered nothing as I quickly put together the lies that would shortly be pouring out of me.

"There are several bunker shelters there. Which two?"

I thanked my lucky stars I had visited.

"Main entrance from the road. On the left. Memorial erected in front of it. That is the most likely. The other bunker is on the right near to the firing range."

"How do we find the *exact* place inside the bunkers?"

"It is at the bottom. Turn to the right side on entering, and look immediately low down on your left. That is what we think. But both places are firmly locked and we are still trying to figure out how to get in."

Then I was shaken again. He held up a very rough version of the design we had been puzzling over for the past couple of weeks.

"Right, just how do you get that idea from this?"

I realised I could not continue the bluff for much longer. Any time now they would realise that I was talking rubbish and could substantiate nothing. Then would come the rough stuff because they really were convinced that I knew.

"We reckoned that would be the only place that one could hide something and recall the exact position at a much later date."

The two of them were getting restive. What the hell could I do to save myself? All I had that might be to my advantage was the possible element of surprise. I was scared stiff and they could certainly see it. The only weapon around was a heavy-looking rubberised truncheon-like torch about a foot long resting on the side of the van opposite me and near to him. Maybe---

"Do you really want to see the way we planned it?" I began to stand up very slowly.

"Yes."

"I think he's lying, Hansie."

"Maybe. But let him talk." He rested the plan down on the small table beside him.

I moved across to the other side of the van. "Hansie" was the more dangerous of the two of them. I was fairly sure the other guy had no weapon. "Well, you see here." I pointed at the centre of the design. "That is the most important symbol."

Hansie bent right over to study it closely. My right hand gripped the heavy torch from behind me and I quickly swung around and hammered it down very hard on the top of his head. He fell heavily down on to the table and then slid to the ground taking the table's contents with him. The other guy immediately leapt at me but I pushed the torch into his face as he came and then kneed him accurately and hard in the groin. He backed away turning slightly and groaning. I hit him across the back of the neck. He fell but was not out. So I made him senseless. One hard kick straight to the jaw.

The gun!

I pulled it from Hansie's pocket and slid it into mine.

The man in the driving seat!

I slid back the door, stepped out into the angry weather and staggered along to the driver's window. He was in there, snugly wrapped around by a thick coat, deeply sleeping and totally unaware. I thought for all of one second. To ensure a safe getaway I had to immobilise him too. I tore open the door, grabbed him by the lapels and, aided by gravity, encouraged him to fall heavily to the ground, bouncing off the step on his way down. The first thing he saw after this rude and painful awakening was me. He tried to get up but I hit him very hard with the gun and then, as quickly as I could manage, dragged and pushed his heavy body back with the other two into the van through the open sliding door.

The rope!

I went in and quickly tied the hands of the three of them behind their backs and together, thankful for yacht master Elizabeth's boat lessons about different knots and their uses. When they came to they would find it difficult to free themselves.

My car keys!

I checked the driver's large pockets. Nothing. Then the small side one. Bingo, they were there! I then collected my wallet, which was now on the van floor, and forced it and my keys together in to my zip-up trouser pocket. Then I rummaged around for the wallets of all three of them. Identification for the police - well, maybe.

My mobile phone!

Gone.

I took Hansie's one and shirt pocketed it. Then looked for the phones of the other two and pocketed those too. The wilds of Dartmoor were almost certainly out of signal range but at least they had nothing to use later if they came to and managed to free themselves.

It was time to go. I exited the van and slid the door to closure behind me. Then I searched for the ignition keys from the driver's cab - and could not find them anywhere.

I was freezing cold and getting very wet. I went quickly back and slid open the door again. Once inside I removed the driver's knotted rope, took off his dry thick coat and put it on. The keys were in the pocket. I flung them out across the moor. The coat was not a bad fit. I buttoned it up. Then I re-secured him. He was breathing heavily and would be unconscious for some time. I moved out and slid the door firmly shut.

I had two options. Stay with the van and keep dry and reasonably warm or get the hell out and find my car which was parked somewhere in the middle of Dartmoor! Despite the freezing cold and driving rain there was not really a choice. May be mad but I simply *had* to get away. They might work themselves loose sooner than I anticipated. And now I badly needed to lie down. I was exhausted.

I squelched my way back out to the tarmac road. Surprisingly the torch still partially worked, flicking on and off, and I arrived there in a couple of minutes. I then turned right and had to follow the road for -- how far? -- five minutes at about twenty miles per hour - one twelfth of twenty - something over a mile and a half. My pace was about a yard, not a metre, and there were one thousand, seven hundred and sixty yards to a mile. I counted as I walked.

The night was now pitch black. Not one star was showing and the wind seemed to be increasing with every step I took, driving the rain into my bare head and face. What concerned me above all was that I was getting very cold. But I trudged on, carefully counting every pace. At one thousand I knew I had gone too far to turn back to the shelter of the van even if I had wanted to. I staggered the next five hundred steps and then started beaming the faltering torchlight downwards looking for tyre marks where my car had been driven off the road. Another two hundred paces and I thought I was going to die. Each pace now was an effort which I tried to see as an achievement.

Soon the unsteady torchlight highlighted some distant bushes. I saw wheel tracks embedded deeply into the soft soil beside me. My heart leapt. I followed the trail off the road with quickened pace and in no time at all *saw my car*.

Had he locked it? I rushed up to the rear door and pulled it. Yes he had. My fingers were frozen but somehow I pulled open the zip, fumbled the key from my pocket and clicked "open." Wonder upon wonder - I heaved back the rear door and flung myself down in to the seat, shutting out the awful weather as I went.

THIRTY-EIGHT

Elizabeth could not sleep.

Her mind kept wandering back to the same problem. Why had he not called her? When away from home he always did, usually at some time in the early evening. It was now two in the morning.

He had said he was staying somewhere on Dartmoor to break his journey back. At first she put the lack of communication down to no mobile coverage for that very rural area. But then if he stayed in a hotel they would always have a land line. So either way he should have communicated with her.

She had tried his mobile phone many times, all to no avail. If he had had an accident she would surely have been informed by now. David, when away, always insisted on calling to say goodnight to Teddy. It was strange - no, worrying - that he had not.

She left the bed yet again, switched on the light and started pacing the room for the third time. Then she seized her mobile phone once more and pushed the button, checking carefully that she was calling the right person. Still no answer. She waited, but there was nothing at the other end.

She decided to call Jonny. Awful thing to do in the middle of the night but she felt in her bones that something was wrong. Terribly wrong! After a long wait he answered.

"Elizabeth. Everything all right?"

"No. Sorry about the time. David always calls without fail when he is away. He hasn't and his mobile does not respond."

"He's probably messed it up. He's done that before."

"Yes but no landline call?"

"Ah, bad sign. Yes. Normally in a hotel. He may well have broken down and is sleeping over in the car. Do you know which way he was coming back?"

"He was going to stay over in some place on Dartmoor."

Jonny had the answer.

"The weather there is horrendous. I saw it on the news. Real south-west rains together with freezing cold. Fairly unusual combination. I reckon he's holed up in the Honda with a mobile that he has either fouled up or there is no coverage where he is. Go to bed and we'll talk first thing tomorrow."

Elizabeth relaxed a little.

"Yes, I hadn't thought of that. Thanks Jonny. You may well be right. Goodness, I hope you are!"

"'Night Elizabeth. Stop worrying."

"Right Jonny. I'll try."

THIRTY-NINE

I lay sprawled across the two back seats of the Honda, freezing cold and gasping for breath, but thankful to have made it. In pretty quick time my thoughts turned from contemplating my imminent demise to trying to stay alive.

Elizabeth always ensured that there was a "survival kit" on board in case the car got stuck on a motorway somewhere. I knew the bag was on the floor behind the passenger seat. I very gingerly reached down, felt around and slowly unzipped it, despite having no feeling in my frozen fingers. Then I trained the torch on it. Inside was a bottle of water, a packet of chocolate biscuits and, taking up most of the space, a blanket which I knew from experience was large enough to cover two people. Fortunately we only once seriously had had to use it.

I then pulled out Hansie's phone from my shirt pocket. It was wet but should still be usable. I studied how it worked – a little different from mine - and, resting on one elbow, fumbled a call home. As I thought, no signal. I tried again but to no avail. I lowered it down between the two seats and then dropped it backwards in to the boot. I followed it with mobiles and wallets which were stuffed uncomfortably in various pockets. I had begun to shiver uncontrollably again.

Bad sign!

Do something!

I knew there were a couple of dry dusters in the front driver's door pocket but closer was the small cloth cover laid across the boot floor. I reached through and grabbed one corner. It came easily. I sat up and used it to dry my soaking hair and face. Then with great difficulty I shed the van driver's coat, incredibly heavy with water, and pushed it aside. All my clothes were soaking wet and freezing cold. They had to come off.

Slowly, slowly, I managed it, the shirt being the most difficult. Socks were removed last. Only my underpants were more or less still dry. Shivering wildly I towelled my naked body as well as possible until I was half dry and then returned the wet cover to the boot. I slowly, very slowly and painfully, pulled the large blanket from the bag and pushed it over on to the passenger seat in the front of the car. Then somehow I found the strength necessary to squeeze myself away from the soaked rear of the car and in between the two front seats and I slumped down into my driver's seat.

Blanket! Blanket!

I could not stop my teeth chattering. Only then did my confused mind think of car heat. I reached behind for the key now resting somewhere on the back seat, grabbed it, and started up. Using the very last reserve of strength I pulled the blanket over to me and wrapped it around myself, felt for the well-known lever and lowered the back of my seat as far as it would go. The awful cold should soon be subsiding. I was not warm but kidded myself that I might be getting less cold as the car heat began to kick in.

I snaked a naked arm behind for the biscuits and prised open the packet. They really tasted good. I felt I hadn't eaten for ages, although I had, and quickly swallowed down four of them. I clicked out the rapidly fading torch and lay it on the passenger seat. Then I slowly made sure each foot was covered and that my shoulders and whole body were inside the blanket. The next thoughts came fast - I pushed the door lock shut beside me. My head. Still wet really. Down the side pocket of the door always in that place were the dusters and my winter hat. I dried my wet hair yet again and then pulled the hat on to my head. There was a flap around which I had never used. I lowered this down over my ears and again checked the blanket.

Now utterly out of energy and bereft of any further thought I turned off the engine to avoid running out of fuel, leaned back and fell into a deep totally exhausted sleep, my ears no longer hearing the noise of the raging rain hammering against the windscreen and my mind oblivious to the now marginally less than extreme cold.

FORTY

Dawn came.

I awoke, confused, until I glanced slowly around.

No-one.

Anywhere.

And no rain.

I was lucky. Maybe I could now think straight. I reckoned I was more or less in a fit state to drive. I had to ride that luck and get away. Far and fast.

I wrapped myself more tightly into the blanket, the seat belt helping, started the engine and then arranged for my shirt, and trousers to be near to the passenger side heating. I then realised I could not drive without shoes and slowly forced my feet into my pair of soggy wet ones. The feeling of this was desperately awful but it simply had to be.

The Civic was not a four wheel drive and it skidded a lot as it made its way slowly around and back across the wet moorland grass. At times when she slid about so much I thought we would not make it, but eventually, after much stopping, starting and high revving, we arrived at the edge of the tarmacked road. I was about to turn right, when a combination of inquisitiveness and a gut feeling that I could be had up for murder if those thugs died, made me contemplate turning left. A couple of vehicles had passed by in the last few minutes. A new day had begun. No, I could not do that. Safety first. I turned right, back the way I had come yesterday and went hell for leather towards Yelverton where there would be mobile coverage and, with luck, safety.

The most urgent thing to do now was to contact Elizabeth who must be worried sick. Shortly I pulled in to the side of the road, one eye constantly viewing the rear mirror, reached back for the nearest mobile phone and called home. It worked. One ring only.

"Hello."

"Morning. Sorry I didn't call yesterday."

"David! Where are you? I've been extremely worried."

"Long story. I was grabbed by thugs asking the whereabouts of the amulet." That brought on a lot of heavy breathing at the other end. "To cut a long story short I have escaped. I am near Yelverton and will be coming back along the M4. Have to tell police as last night I left three men tied up in their van and they will need food and drink by now."

"This leads to Jessica and all that. Not the police - ambulance instead!"

"Yes, of course!" She was right. "Must go. May call again later."

"Be very, very careful. I love you. Come straight home!"

"Believe me I will. ' Bye love."

I called 999 and asked for an ambulance to help three men who were ill in a red and green van. I explained exactly where they were and said it was urgent, then cut the call before they could process my details, lowered the window and threw the phone into a small pond that had formed nearby.

Then it was all systems go for the motorway. At the first petrol station I came to I pulled in to the far obscured side, dressed quickly in damp clothes, filled up with petrol, bought a coffee and sandwich, and was about to go non-stop for home when I remembered the gun! I extracted it from deep in my pocket and had a look. I was horrified to see it was fully loaded! I removed the small bullets and stretched over and hid them and the gun in the passenger door pocket.

Then I was away at top speed.

FORTY-ONE

Elizabeth called Jonny and gave him the few details she had learned of my experiences. Jonny in turn passed on the information to Piet and that was where the maximum disquiet was felt. Piet called Jessica and spoke immediately she answered.

"Jessica, I'm coming over. Dave seems to have been accosted by three men talking about the amulet. One of them had a South African accent!"

"Oh my God! How on earth? Where was he?"

"Plymouth. Way down in the west country seeing clients. We must talk. We may all soon be in some difficulty."

"Yes, please come. See you soon."

In a matter of minutes Piet had arrived and she let him in.

"How on earth ----?"

He put his finger to his lips. "We don't yet know but it is only you who can have any inkling about how they are on to us."

"I've been thinking about it. There is only one possible place. Walvis Bay. Karl Winkler *seemed* to be a really good guy. He was the only one to know anything of my story. Somehow it has got out and been picked up by real undesirables. I'm feeling really scared. And how is David?"

"He's all right. Elizabeth did not know the full story but he is on his way home and not stopping anywhere."

"I've really started something. I thought this amulet thing was simply a relic from history." She looked deeply distressed. "I think you might like a beer or something?"

"After the preliminaries, yes please."

"Preliminaries?"

"We didn't greet each other."

She laughed and gave him a gentle hug. He did not let her go. "I care for you a lot Jessica. We've been through all sorts of things in a very short time. If this blows up into anything I'm with you. Remember that!"

He let her go but she stayed, putting her arms around him.

"I feel things for you too. Feelings I was always trained to ignore. And I have always stuck to that."

They stayed silently close for a full three minutes. Then Piet let out a shout.

"Coffee, not beer! That was really what I came for. Not all this lovey-dovey nonsense."

She smiled, released herself and went into the tiny kitchen.

Piet slid down in one of the two comfortable chairs as the trolley arrived. Not just coffee but cake as well. Jessica sat opposite him in the other seat.

"You do realise that this place is where I held up Dave and Elizabeth at gunpoint?"

"Yes. If you recall I phoned in and did not get any vibes to indicate things were horribly wrong. But that's all history now. It seems we have a big problem on our hands with David's experiences. We'll hear all about it all tomorrow. What was this man Winkler like?"

"Harmless and very friendly. I'd swear on it. And he certainly did not entertain the Nazi views of his father."

"It would have been a great story to tell to a mate somewhere." Piet munched the delicious sponge.

"Anything German around where you were travelling?"

"Well yes! I asked for directions to Winkler's house from a cook in the place where some of the menus I saw on the wall were in German. Not surprising really. It is well known that some Germans reside in the country. But surely there can be no connection there?" She looked incredulous.

"Residual Nazism maybe. I know that the South African Broederbond were a bit that way inclined. But I thought those sympathies had worn off long ago. So what do we do if these same people follow up on us? Very likely they know of you and may well come at us after failing to get what they wanted with David."

"I think I can look after myself. But I am worried about everyone I've brought into this mess."

"Don't even think about that. They are all pretty switched on. We can't do much until David tells us the worst. However I do not think you should be on your own, just in case."

"How do you mean?"

"Don't take this the wrong way, Jessica, but I think I should move in to the spare room. Elizabeth agrees. I have already asked her if she minded having two in her flat. She thinks it would be a really good precaution."

"Well, Piet, nice idea. I would welcome another person here. Would help with safety for a while." She remained quietly thinking for a while. "But remember I've never been really close to a man and now is not the time."

Piet had expected exactly that. "Ok I promise to keep off and behave like a monk. We will face this situation together and hope it does not escalate. Move in tomorrow?"

"Yes. I'll talk to Elizabeth and make up the spare room bed. Thanks very much." She finished her coffee.

"I'll go. See you then about midday. Call me if anything erupts in the meantime. And do not let anyone in unless you are sure of them."

He stood up, walked to the door, blew her a kiss and let himself out.

FORTY-TWO

I arrived back in Hove that evening. The going had been hard as it frequently rained and the large amount of traffic demanded total concentration. I was utterly shattered and staggered in to the house, blinded by the lighting. Elizabeth was shocked to see my condition and immediately ran a bath into whose water I thankfully sank. The warmth penetrated my very bones and quickly righted quite a few bodily pains. After that it was large amounts of hot soup, a short chat about Teddy, and then, on Elizabeth's no nonsense instruction, straight into bed. I slept right through to the following morning, for once totally unaware of the woman beside me.

Over breakfast I told her my story. She wanted all the detail and I related everything. She became more and more thoughtful as the words unfolded and eventually came to their inevitable much-still-to-be-sorted-out end.

"You are lucky to be alive!" She was looking very shocked.

"Yes. I realised soon enough that I was on my own and that these were bloody desperate men. I am surprised that things worked out as they did as I'm not known for my fisticuff skills! We must tell Piet and Jessica all about it. They are intertwined with the whole thing and could now be in some danger."

"Done. I gave them the gist of our phone conversation. Piet is moving in to the Pimlico flat's spare room. The two of them are taking full precautions - well, as many as possible in the circumstances. And so should we."

"Great! She could well have a visit from them at any time. Piet must have realised that those thugs got to me through Jessica. There is simply no other way."

"Agreed. We must *all* be very careful. Maybe even drop the whole thing? But we can talk about that later. I have arranged for Piet, Jessica and Jonny to be sure to be in the office tomorrow. You must have today to rest up. But can still be stopped if you do not feel up to it."

"Great. No need to cancel. I'm feeling fine after that full night's sleep. Tomorrow we need to have a very careful examination of what is going on and how it impinges on all of us. But no blame on Jessica who is probably feeling bloody awful about the whole thing. Somehow she has been incredibly hoodwinked."

FORTY-THREE

"Urgent phone for you, Sir."

Agetha DuPlessis was pleased that Aiden Kriel took the call quickly from her. The man at the other end seemed very agitated.

"Kriel speaking."

"Hansie here." He spoke in Afrikaans to avoid being understood by any Brit who may be listening in.

"All well? Where are you?"

"Big trouble Aiden! We are very much in your hands. We zeroed in on the leader in London and then spent ages tracking him to Dartmoor. We ambushed him in the best isolated place there and were extracting details of you know what when the bastard completely surprised us and escaped."

"What, all three of you? How on earth could he do that? Did you catch him?"

"No. He bloody tricked us. Spur of the moment surprise and then he tied us up and left us. Must have called an ambulance which arrived hours later. He probably was worried he might kill us and there would be repercussions that would come from that. I simply do not know how his mind worked. The medics freed us but after assessing the situation they told us to wait while they called the police. We immediately overpowered them, took the ambulance, drove to Yelverton, and ditched it. Then hiked all the way, often in the pouring rain, from there to Plymouth, and so far we've managed to avoid detection."

"But---"

"No questions *please.* Just listen. We are holed up in the New Continental Hotel. We have limited cash, cards or weaponry. Just the clothes we stand up in. He took all our wallets and phones. We are in very urgent need of money transferred to us here to pay for this hotel and our travel. We have to avoid arousing any interest in us. I am uncertain how to proceed and have to be very careful to avoid a whole retinue of people who by now must be very much on the warpath."

Aiden Kriel had quickly brought up a picture of where they were on to his screen. He was appalled at their predicament and knew that action was needed fast. Recriminations could come later. They had to be got out to avoid any possibility of their activities being examined and understood. As the most senior South African person in their secretive organisation he knew things that they didn't.

"Passports?"

"Yes, we have them. They were in a pocket of the van door. At least he knew nothing about *them*!"

Kriel breathed a little more easily when he heard that. "Hansie. Listen carefully. Stay incognito where you are in the hotel. Eat, sleep and be normal. More than sufficient money will arrive probably later today, if not it will be early tomorrow. Plan your quickest and safest journeys back to Jo'burg and get out of the country as soon as is sensible and safe. Under *no* circumstances get yourselves caught."

"Are you sure of this, Aiden? You can actually get cash to us?" The beseeching tone of his voice reflected his deep anxiety.

"Certain. You presumably have false names and a room number there?"

"Yes. Mine is James Brown. Room 231."

Right. Stay put. You will be contacted."

"How Aiden?"

"Just try to relax. Keep someone in your room at all times of the day and night."

And with that he put down the phone.

Aiden Kriel did his sums in American currency. Three hotel rooms for, say, two nights. Three train fares to London and three flight costs to South Africa. Say two thousand five hundred dollars. Doubled to five thousand dollars. Call that five thousand pounds to allow for unforeseen events.

There existed a chain of very top "Nazi" leaders in most countries. A residue of hatred sealed into the brains of those few who were still besotted by the idea of a future uprising. All of these elite leaders were of course completely unknown to the world at large or even to their own country's extremely ugly organisation to which they each belonged. Every leader was only to be contacted in high emergency situations. They knew each other but there was rarely any getting together or acknowledgement to anyone that they existed.

Kriel had realised immediately he had on his hands one of those desperate scenarios with which he must deal *now*. He code emailed his British opposite number who carried the innocent sounding name of Alexander Ashton. This man was anything but! Brainwashed into the extreme Jackboot level of British society at a very young age he soon realised that the only way forwards for their endeavours was to go underground, stay silent, and find like minds around the world.

Steadily over the years he ferreted out others of the same persuasion, although sorting the genuine from the casual was always tricky. As time passed he had grown a British team of rabid Nazi believers and over the same period had been accepted in to the small group of international below-the-radar very top leaders. They all looked forward to the day when the Aryan race would again rise up. It simply had to be.

Kriel and Ashton knew each other, both having risen out of the ranks over the years and both being possessed by the same ideologies. The Afrikaner relayed the story as he knew it and asked for the money to go quickly to the hotel by hand. His men must get out of England fast. Also, if possible, he asked Ashton to learn from the three men whatever detail they knew of the amulet project and, if possible, follow up with his own team and keep in touch on the subject.

In just a few minutes the coded reply arrived.

"Will comply. Delivery will be tonight. Hope to obtain all detail and act. Help will be given to bring about their safe return home. Will keep in touch."

FORTY-FOUR

Everyone arrived early. I had decided on the line I was going to take but had to hold fire listening to an understandably downcast Jessica.

"I'm so sorry to have brought this with me, Dave. They obviously have somehow followed through from my trip to Walvis Bay. I really had no idea---"

"That's enough. We are dealing with a real bunch of criminals. We will not go anywhere near to our police. That *would* make life difficult for us all, not just you, Jessica. We took this on in good faith and, I guess, we will see it through. Precautions all round though. These guys may seek out any one of us and try to beat us into supplying the whereabouts of that amulet. But my guess is they will be keeping their heads down. So take great care. In the meantime we continue the search? Anyone disagree?"

There was no dissent.

Piet muttered, "With you all the way." And the four others solemnly nodded their heads.

At that moment there was a knock on the door and in came a grinning Giles Rathbury with coffee for us all. "The vibes seemed to tell me this might be useful!" He carefully lowered the tray and left.

I carried on talking whilst Elizabeth distributed the mugs.

"Alex and the Singapore appointment goes ahead. Piet, you are seeing Global again. Life must go on as normally as possible."

"During which time we take Kenley airport apart."

"Correct, Jonny, but, having been there and seen the huge sprawl of the airfield, I do wonder where we start."

"We have to *solve* this." A heretofore silent Elizabeth directed a beam of light. "What you see must be understood." And up on the wall came Jessica's plan.

"So far we are sure of only three things." She measured her words carefully. "The triangle is England and the K is for Kenley. The amulet shown with a neck chain is what we seek. Other than that we think the cross is not necessarily representing a church because of its unusual "square" shape but are still uncertain. The two lines with balloons - any ideas? Big mystery. INN, don't know. The rectangle at the bottom could be any part of the airfield or a place of worship, with that shaped open area and then some way beneath that lies the buried amulet. I think we should all spend time together walking the place. The penny might eventually drop with one of us."

"I realise it is a huge area but what about metal detection equipment? You cannot go around digging up anything and everything. I believe the amulet has gold and silver in it and is presumably in a box of some kind, hopefully metal?"

"Good thinking Piet." I, too, had been pondering digging.

"However, people, maybe police, certainly airfield authorities, whoever they are, would all be closely interested in such activity."

"Then do it at night!"

"Piet we work all day! When do we sleep?" Elizabeth already pursued a busy life.

I realised that it was time to summarise things.

"I think we should go back to square one first. Let's all look up everything we can find relating to the Kenley airfield - buildings, dates, the situation as it was in war time. All that sort of thing. Then sometime later back here to compare results. Piet, can you come up with detail on metal detection - price, suppliers and how you work the damned things?"

He nodded agreement.

"Oh and there is an organisation called Kenley Revival. They might be able to help us in some way. Trouble is we don't want them to get any inkling of what we are about. And don't let us all approach them at once!"

I looked around. Brains were reappraising. It was a good time to get back to our normality.

"OK everybody. Meeting over. Keep thinking about what's up on the wall. Solving that would help a lot. Time now to get back to work. Two days for the next get-together. Same time, same place."

FORTY-FIVE

The money arrived all in notes that same evening - fifties, twenties and tens. It was nine o'clock and the three South Africans, having had a meal delivered to Room 231, were munching away together. There was a gentle tap on the door. All three jumped up.

Anticipation?

Fear?

Police?

Hotel staff?

Or the one they really wanted?

Hansie gingerly opened up.

Alexander Ashton moved in and quickly pushed the door shut behind him. He had a case in his left hand. One look at these three men told him he was in the right place, a feeling that was instantly confirmed by his accent when Hansie spoke.

"Good evening. My name is James Brown."

Ashton smiled. "And mine is Nelson Mandela."

Any remaining doubt melted away at once and he was ushered in to the room's fourth chair. Never had an unknown visitor anywhere been so welcome. They were all extremely worried that they might go to prison in the United Kingdom for a mighty long time. This man could maybe save them.

"Would you like a beer, Nelson?" Van driver smiled and pointed to some bottles.

"Yes please. But I must stay only for a short time." He paused and took a deep breath. Then spoke quietly.

"First I must give you this. Five thousand pounds exactly. I suggest for safety that you pocket one third each. After you have settled the hotel bill tomorrow morning take a taxi to Plymouth Station where you can purchase tickets to London. Once there take a taxi to Heathrow airport. Book on to the first available plane home." He placed the money on a small table beside the bottle of beer that had been put there and met the eyes of all three.

"Cheers."

They all joined in with that. Before there was time to thank this stranger for the money his voice had changed to staccato and his face took on a hardened look.

"This is all very, very dangerous. I have to leave in ten minutes maximum. And you *must* get out tomorrow. In the time we have here please tell me all you know of the amulet. We will carry on the good work after you have left, as requested by your Mr Kriel."

At the mention of that name they knew they were truly with a high-powered character. One of their own. Aiden had successfully fixed the whole thing. Exceeding slightly the time allotted they relayed their story to him, giving particular attention to details they had learned of the amulet's whereabouts. Then they handed over a photocopy of the plan showing clues which they had so far failed to understand.

Ashton's face showed nothing but his heart raced as it dawned on him that they were now well down the track to a find. He pocketed the paperwork and memorised everything else. No words which they spoke were to be committed to paper or mobile. There must, as always, be no record anywhere.

When every detail had been passed over, and questions answered, he rose, shook hands all round, wished them a safe journey, and was about to leave the room when he turned quickly around.

"I nearly forgot. Car details. That guy in the Honda. I would like his name, car registration number, address and anything else you may know?"

They looked blank. But Van driver saved the day. He felt deep down in his pocket. "I took the car's insurance cover details, just in case. Sort of instinct." He handed over the single sheet of paper. Ashton snatched and very carefully pocketed it, and went quickly out and down in the lift, quietly and almost unnoticed through the hotel ground floor and out in to the dark night.

Not seen.

Not heard.

He had never been there.

In a couple of minutes he was driving his Jaguar away from the parking he had found just outside the hotel and back home to Birmingham. The lengthy journey would give him plenty of time to think.

FORTY-SIX

Back in Pimlico Jessica was preparing the evening meal. Piet had returned and was checking the security of the flat. The front door was locked and had been strengthened considerably since that time when Haffenbacker, accompanied by Jessica, then known as Marguerite, had smashed their way in. The windows were all locked but glass could, of course, be broken. Albeit not noiselessly.

"Liver and bacon and I hope you like it!"

She laid the small table while Piet arranged the two chairs. She then brought it out and they sat down together.

"Oh heck. I forgot. The wine." Piet reached out for the one bottle of red that he had already opened and poured. "Cheers. Here's to a successful conclusion of the amulet search."

Jessica drank and then looked at him wistfully.

"I now fervently wish I had not become involved with the whole darned thing. It has brought nothing but trouble, particularly to Dave. Just look at what he went through. He could have been killed."

"In a way it's my fault. Getting you out of that prison. It was really simply a question of my inquisitiveness at the time." He smiled mischievously. "Maybe I should have left well alone!"

"You saved my life. I would have died had there been no way out. You *know* that." She smiled. "I hope you like the meal. I'm a trained spy, not a cook."

"It's marvellous. Back in Pretoria I normally heat up something from the supermarket and leave it at that.

Pretty boring at times. So tell me, are you eventually going back to France?"

Jessica had a momentary vision of the idyllic life followed by her mother and sister. A lot more sunshine was there and the glorious sea was nearby. Father had had a boat in which they visited the resorts along the south coast. It had been sold when he had died at an untimely age. She had missed out on much of the fun and games due to having been sucked into the small, very up-market, women's section of the Direction-Generale de la Securite Interieur in Paris. That organisation eventually had absorbed her life totally and she had lost touch with normal things. What she would give now to be safely back with them, free of all the baggage with which recent history had saddled her.

"I suppose I will once this is all sorted out. I still have the right documentation to get me back in to my own country!"

"Where you will be known as Marguerite?"

"Yes." She concentrated on her liver and bacon.

Just then Piet's mobile vibrated against his chest. He looked. It was Elizabeth.

"Just checking that all is well. I'm a little nervous about the whole situation. Call us immediately if anything strange occurs, particularly if you have someone trying to get in!"

"Ok Elizabeth. We will do that. I trust you will do the same with us if you have any problems too. At least we are all prepared for the possibility of some sort of unwanted visit."

"Yes, that's good. Sleep well, despite the circumstances." She rang off. They finished their meal, cleared the table and sat down. It was time to go over the safety arrangements. Piet, surprisingly, was fairly laid back about it all.

"I'm pretty sure they will not come here. More likely to try and find Dave again, although they will have to be careful. He could have been to the police who might just be waiting to pounce on them."

"Agreed. But we, too, must be cautious. That door is now very difficult to break down. The windows are all bolted and any way in through them will be very noisy! And that is it really."

"Well, not quite." He smiled.

"What am I missing?"

"Mobiles on and within easy reach."

"But of course. We then have to bring in the police, but no way will I be going back to my South African imprisonment."

"Sorry, forgot. We call Dave straight away. And deal with intruders ourselves. No police. They will forage into both our recent pasts and that will be fatal." Their personal defence right now? He remembered seeing a hockey stick in the corner of his room.

Jessica rose. "I'm going to wash up. I suggest you have the bathroom first. I'll follow on. And let us hope all will be well and we wake up tomorrow to a lovely peaceful day."

FORTY-SEVEN

The air was thick with possibilities, or so it seemed to Alexander Ashton. The missing amulet, so long sought after by the world's Hitlerites, could be within his grasp. It would rocket propel his elevation amongst his fellow elite Nazis. That amulet meant so much. It had powers of persuasion for the young, in his view simply because it embodied a direct link to the Fuhrer. Many believers were convinced that the object itself was somehow possessed of magical strengths. Either way it was an extremely important device.

He was no longer a young buck. Yesterday's return drive to to and from Plymouth had left him exhausted and he had slept most of the morning. His wife, Hilda, had sensed that something was going on but had questioned nothing. She spent the time he was sleeping doing some much needed shopping in the nearby Bull Ring, which she always enjoyed. Lunch was ready when at last he came downstairs.

"Sorry to have upset the routine." He kissed the back of her head as he moved to his seat at the table.

"It has to be important. I know you only too well!"

Hilda was fifty-five years of age and exuded an aura of attractive solidity. Slightly greying hair somehow enhanced her good looks and, given her firm body, she presented every inch the best of German womanhood. She was also the grand-daughter of Himmler's right hand officer, a staunch believer, and the only person in Britain who was fully aware of her husband's fearsome (most Brits would say loathsome) international credentials.

"For your ears only, my dear." And he spent the lunch time telling her his whole story.

She listened carefully to every detail. At the end of it all she exploded.

"Good heavens! *The* amulet! We *must* find it."

"We will. Tonight I will summon the organisation's two most loyal and trustworthy men and brief them. First they will have to recce the airfield. Then plan a break-in followed by a lot of wall bashing and other investigation."

"Be very careful. Security at airfields can be strong."

"Yes I know. But the spitfires and hurricanes for which it became famous departed a very long time ago. They train a few cadets there now in gliding techniques. Otherwise the whole place is also being used as a permanent war memorial."

"And if you find it - the amulet?" She looked questioningly at him.

"I will inform the elite. Nobody else. They may come up with ideas. We will have to preserve it very carefully for use as and when the Rising comes. We all know it will happen, but we have no way of knowing when. Maybe the jewel will help and guide us all."

Both had finished their steak and onions without really appreciating them, such was the impact of his revelations. Alexander pulled the sketch from his pocket and passed it across to her. "This is the detail of where the amulet is hidden. It in no way immediately relates to what I have heard from the South Africans about what they learned about the hiding place. You might bring your mind to work on it and see what you come up with."

Her eyes immediately registered his written word "Kenley."

"So *that* really is the place. The Luftwaffe pulverised the airfield there in the good old days." She cast her eye over the remaining clues before carefully pocketing the document. "I will do some thinking. If you do not achieve anything this piece of paper may be the only rung left on your mystery ladder."

"Absolute mute." He placed one hand on hers.

"Absolute mute." She murmured.

That was their lifelong mantra whose words they had always used in situations such as this. Not a whisper of what had just passed between them would ever get out.

Anywhere.

At any time.

FORTY-EIGHT

The moment I awoke the following morning I called Piet.

"All well there?"

"Yes thanks, Dave, no unwanted intruders. Good night's sleep actually."

"Great. I think we must have a closer, in depth, look at Kenley, don't you? Saves having another interminable meeting!"

"Funny you should say that. I am already in touch with a number of metal detection people. There are devices that can tell you about the presence of almost any type of metal - gold, silver, iron and steel. We really do need to poke around there a bit."

"Great, you're ahead of me. I was going to suggest that all four of us visit the airfield next Wednesday, splitting up and just having an initial look around everywhere keeping in mind all the time those sketched out clues we are finding so difficult to interpret. Jonny has said he will hold the fort in the office."

"Yep, ok Dave. I'll arrange things with Jessica - oh, here she is fixing breakfast. We have three days to prepare everything for the visit. Work can wait!"

"Agreed. Speak soon. Enjoy the breakfast. Continental, no doubt?"

"I'm about to find out. Cheers."

And that was it. I turned around to find Elizabeth had been listening to the whole conversation.

"Eavesdropping?"

"Self-interest. Good to know what we are doing next!"

"I was going to discuss with you."

She smiled. "You are entirely right. We go on Wednesday. No other meetings on the subject until then. I have one or two more ideas on the sketch but need to explore it all further at the site. Are you sure there was no security there when you visited?"

"None. Not surprising really as very little activity seems to take place even though it is still a "designated Ministry of Defence airfield."

"So we need a ground picture to follow."

"Of course. I have printed off plans of the whole place. Being so huge it is probably best if we initially select areas to check. Piet and presumably Jessica will be trying out metal detection in the most likely places. You never know they might just hit the jackpot. I think you and I should walk the site noting the most likely spots that could have been in use seventy odd years ago during the war. We will have to establish ways to get into the various bunkers around the place---"

And take a look at the old firing range. What on earth was that for?"

"In case the airfield was raided I think. The resident pilots and serving people had to be weapon ready. Maybe German paratroopers? Could be anything. Horrid thought isn't it?"

"Breakfast time - hungry or not?"

I did not reply. She had turned on her heel and made for the kitchen as Teddy came noisily jumping his way down the stairs.

FORTY-NINE

Wednesday was cold but at least it was not wet. The forecast said dry all day. We considered ourselves lucky as, fortified with warm clothing, we all four had arrived at the Kenley airfield in the early morning. The boot was crammed full of metal detecting equipment, a strong spade, a couple of flasks of coffee and a large box of sandwiches. I parked the Honda near to the swing gate entrance as before and we clambered out.

Following our plan, Elizabeth and I made for the small perimeter road while Piet and Jessica carried in two of the metal detectors and moved towards the first long bunker which was the centrepiece of the whole area. At that time of the morning there were a couple of dog walkers and one brave scantily clad runner some distance away. Otherwise no-one. We more or less had the place to ourselves.

Elizabeth was the self-appointed photographer, although we all had mobile phones and I straightway took a few pictures of the vast airfield runways. Then she and I began our two mile walk around the whole perimeter and deviations from it. We noted everything that could in any way be of relevance to our investigation. Each long blast pen was investigated. Most entrances were double padlocked, and all looked totally derelict. Clearly nobody had been in and out for some time. Maybe Piet would manage some metallic registration around the entrances but there was no way at present that he could get in.

We moved on around the perimeter road to the weather station. Had it been there during the war? If not there was no point in looking more closely at it. Something we had to find out. We trudged slowly onwards, encouraged to keep moving by the cold wind which was punishing us in the same way that it was dealing with the two windsocks which were at full stretch. We then arrived at what we thought was the old officers mess. We would have to check that this building was actually there during the war, otherwise no need to investigate it. I thought it likely that it was so and any confirmation and would lead us on to a huge and tricky job. First we had to get in. Then explain what we were doing and, inevitably, what we sought.

Onwards, now directly into the freezing wind and fighting madly to stay upright, to the buildings where the gliders were housed. Probably all fairly new - but, if so, what was there before? Elizabeth captured it all in pictures. Just then a couple more runners moved past us, gallantly fighting the elements. They were dressed similarly in shorts and tee-shirts and had to keep seriously running just to stay moderately warm. The leader kept consulting his watch, their timing being all-important and cutting out most other thought. Clearly there was no interest in us at all. We then passed some pretty modern residential houses which abutted the airfield before arriving at the lower level firing range.

Here we stopped awhile. This place was top of the list of areas to search. We had considered it just the sort of construction which could have been used as a place for anything one wished to hide. It was now dilapidated but had many points at which something small could have been concreted in. We desperately tried to find anything in its surroundings which could be related to the plan we had so frequently deeply studied. But no luck. There was simply nothing which fitted. We scrambled our way back up to the perimeter road.

We had now almost completed the tortuous trip. I spent some time looking at a couple of the information boards, shaped like aircraft wings and standing perhaps six feet high showing pictures of aircrew who had died doing their duty. It was very sobering reading and a very fitting memorial.

We descended the steps leading out, grabbed the coffee and sandwiches from the car boot and quickly lowered ourselves inside the Honda to escape the biting wind. I produced a small notebook and we noted down all we had seen and our observations at each stage of our journey around the place. A few minutes later the other two arrived, shoved their hardware into the car boot, got in and quickly slammed shut the rear doors.

"Bloody freezing! Coffee please."

South African Piet felt the cold more than most.

"Yes, good to be back. Did you come across anything interesting?" Elizabeth, keen to come away with something, uttered the question as she unscrewed the first thermos flask.

"No, but as we said this is just the beginning. We've jotted down details of certain areas to be looked at again and taken a few pictures of things, but we must get into those bunkers. I would say in there somewhere is a very likely place for something to be hidden. Who knows, our German friend might even have been involved in their construction."

"No, I don't think so. The guy was brought over here near to the end of the war. These blast pens must have been built fast and much earlier." I was pretty sure of that one.

We quickly finished off the second flask of coffee as we ate up the sandwiches. Shortly afterwards I began the drive back into central London. The car had rapidly warmed up. One could think coherently again. But I did not think we had achieved much. Nothing, just nothing, really seemed to fit.

.

FIFTY

That evening Piet took Jessica out to a restaurant he knew in Piccadilly that was famous for its Mediterranean cooking. Italian, French, maybe Greek foods were all were represented. Somewhat to his amusement Jessica ordered French onion soup and beef bourguignon. Perhaps a cry for her real origins. He doubled up with her and then ordered a red wine.

"What a lovely place. Just like home!"

Jessica was excited by this super taste of civilisation. She had come back into the real world at a time when she had almost given up all hope.

"I've been here a couple of times when over from South Africa. I thought you might like it."

"Like it!! It is wonderful. You know I still get nightmares when I think about that place in Johannesburg. I cannot go back. I really would rather die."

The wine arrived. Piet swirled and tasted it and nodded his acceptance. He too had memories and tried to help her. "It will probably take some time for you to relax back in to normal life. My recollection of your incarceration is still pretty vivid too, despite not being inside as a prisoner myself. Getting back into France is the best and probably only idea for you I think."

"Yes."

"But your links here?"

"Oh, as Lady Banforth you mean?"

"Well, yes."

The soup arrived. She noted that the ingredients looked correct - unusual for most English establishments.

Piet raised his glass.

"Cheers."

Their glasses touched.

"Well, actually there is no Lady Banforth. I linked with the elderly noble Lord for an occasion when he needed a partner. He asked me to move in to the manor house for a while to appear with him at some of his "functions." I only agreed as it gave me better access to the British financial great and good which I needed for my somewhat doubtful work with the Haffenbacker organisation. He didn't know about any of that of course!"

"You do have a vivid past Jessica. Almost as tangled up as I am with this cheese in my soup!"

"Patience Piet. It soon unravels."

"Presumably your French passport is in your maiden name and valid?"

"Yes."

"Your one way out of all this?"

"Yes."

"And never to come back?"

"Well, not for years. I would like things to calm right down before I travel anywhere outside France."

"Would you go back to your Securite Interieur people? Sorry I have forgotten the full name."

"No! Good heavens, No! Leaving them in the way I did was just never done. The Haffenbacker crowd seemed attractive to me at the time. I wish now, of course, that I had left well alone. They turned out to be simply a high grade bunch of crooks."

At that point the main course arrived and their conversation ceased. The bourguignon looked delicious. Their glasses were replenished.

As the waiter left Piet continued his questioning about her future. Beneath it all he was anxious but tried not to show it. He was going to lose her and there seemed little he could do to remedy the situation.

"So as soon as the amulet thing is settled you will be off back to la belle France then?"

"Mais oui, I suppose so."

"And I will be off back to Pretoria and will never see you again."

"Unless you are ever in France. I could show you around the beautiful south of my country."

They continued talking at some length about their recent past experiences in South Africa. All too soon they were at the end of the meal and it was time to go. Piet settled up and they made their way out to look for a taxi back to Pimlico.

FIFTY-ONE

"I don't want to lose you Jessica."

They were back in the flat and Piet was growing increasingly anxious. In fact, desperate. He had been through a huge self-examination on the journey back. What did his future life hold? Where was it all going? He was so engrossed with his thoughts that he almost forgot to pay the driver.

The evening, the super food, the surroundings. It was all enveloping her in a way she had never before experienced. And, of course, although she could hardly explain it to herself and wasn't really trying to do so, she had been strongly drawn to him. Her reply, contradicting everything she thought she was, just came out.

"I feel that way too but----"

That was enough for him. A near madness had taken over. He took her in his arms.

She didn't resist.

He kissed her wildly.

She initially made no effort to stop him but then gasped out, "This is no good Piet. I explained to you. I have never gone near any man like this. I've always kept away. You know that!"

"Well, *not* this time."

"What do you mean?"

Throwing caution to the winds he picked her up and carried her in to her room, kicked shut the door and lowered her carefully down on to her bed.

FIFTY-TWO

Our business was getting into a bit of a mess. We were spending too much time away from it working on all that Jessica had brought to us. I was keen to get things back on track. Piet was at last despatched to Global to have the second chat they had requested. Alex and Sonya were ready to leave for Singapore. We had lengthy talks about the work they would be doing, visits back to us approximately every three months, and all the other detail related to their work. They were to leave in a couple of days.

Later I followed up on Piet's visit with a quick call in to see Walt at Global. Everything was still well there. Meanwhile Elizabeth brought the accounts up to date together with all the personnel requirements needed to keep us legal. All in all we had a pretty frenetic few days keeping up with things. It was only in bed at night that I could get a clear enough mind to consider our next move. One was able to concentrate there, free from all the daily business routines and accompanying noise.

I lay on my back and stared up into the darkness. Elizabeth was breathing gently beside me. A schedule of visits to the airfield was necessary. Who was to go? On which date? And which area that day would they use to investigate everything in minute detail. Oh, and the best time of day for avoiding onlookers. Again the vision of the plan that had been brought back by Jessica raised its ugly head. Any link between it and Kenley airfield had completely eluded us. Best not to think---

The house phone rang! Who on earth? At this time of night? I yanked myself out of bed and staggered downstairs, sensing half way down that Elizabeth was following.

I saw it was Jonny.

"Hi there."

"Dave, Jonny."

"What on earth? At this time of night?"

"Dave, turn on the BBC TV News programme."

"Are they on now?"

"Go to channel 231. Quick!"

And he hung up.

Elizabeth got to the television set before me. In seconds we were seeing and listening.

"---seen disappearing in a Mercedes car which the police have confirmed had false number plates. The men were reported to have been running from the scene. Two large holes have been made in two of the airfield's historic bunkers, the padlocked entrance doors having first been blown open. There seems to be no reason for this action, other than vandalism, to an airfield which is being kept intact as a war memorial."

The newscaster continued on with another subject and Elizabeth straightway closed down. We looked long and hard at each other. She zeroed in to the situation immediately.

"Is that the place you told them on your Dartmoor foray?"

"Yes. I was lying of course. Simply self-protection at the time. They were about to knock hell out of me to get to the truth."

"Then they probably found nothing at the airfield."

My mind was reeling. Where would this whole thing be leading now?

"Correct."

"So there's not a problem. Things go on as before."

"They could come for me again, still thinking I know of the damned amulet's whereabouts."

"Oh I really do hope not!"

"You are probably right. The publicity will have scared them off."

"Let's assume so. Do we phone everyone now and let them know?"

"Not at all! Back to bed young lady. We need our sleep."

FIFTY-THREE

"The bloody idiots!"

Alexander Ashton screamed at the late night television news. His chosen collaborators had certainly done the job but he had just been informed from the fleeing car that nothing had been found after the explosions had taken place on the Kenley airfield.

"Did they even damned well look?" This normally composed man was actually shouting at his wife.

"Calm down, Alex. I've never seen you like this before. It is important. Of course. But you know they may not have missed the amulet. Very likely it wasn't there and people have been misrepresenting things all the way through. The question is now will the four of them in the car get safely away?"

"Yes. Any second now it will be securely garaged in the outskirts of Croydon and dismantled. Plates were false so that was covered. But that's not the point. We have completely and utterly failed."

"And the next move?" Hilda was trying hard was calm him down.

"Eyes open, mouths shut as usual. We should normally sit back and let this whole thing pass over. But right now I feel I simply cannot do that. We are *that* close to the amulet, the greatest treasure in our cause. We need all of its mystical powers at this difficult time. In it is enshrined the spirit of all we stand for."

Hilda breathed it out. "Make *sure* you really do remember the number one rule on silence, my dear!"

"Yes, of course, but this situation *cannot* rest at the moment. I have a fall back plan, worked on night and day, and I will now steadily see it through. If that fails, then, ok, we sit tight. When all is over I will report back to my opposite number in South Africa, to let him know the worst. Or maybe, by then, the best. What a *hell* of a mess!"

Hilda, the very practical Nazi, retired to the kitchen to make him an Ovaltine drink. The state he was in needed careful treatment. His idea of a fall back plan disturbed her deeply. He might not sleep very well but the drink would certainly help.

The following morning all had changed.

Anger had gone. Discipline had taken its place. Over breakfast Alexander passed her a copy of the Honda driving licence and the Johnston home address.

Hilda understood at once.

"You are going there?"

"Next few days, yes."

"They won't tell you where to find the amulet. Probably having awful trouble themselves."

"They will know more than we do. And we can make them talk!" Alexander bristled. He knew how.

"My function?" Hilda knew she might be needed.

"If all goes wrong carry out the Plan - fast!" This was simply a way of ridding the house of any Nazi connection, mainly paperwork and computer records, in a matter of minutes.

"How will I know?"

"The H H warning. One way or another I will see that a message gets through to you quickly."

"So my function is simply to sit here and wait."

"Yes, Hilda."

She made a face. "Disliked but understood. And after that I visit you in jail or wherever they decide to keep you?" She crunched heavily on her remaining corn flakes.

He stood up, moved behind her, and kissed her on the head as he passed by. "Just going to arrange a few things. The real action will start from tomorrow onwards. Everything will be all right. Have I ever failed yet?"

And with that he was gone.

FIFTY-FOUR

Detective Constable Nicole Sheppard had entered the Devon and Cornwall police service straight from university. Her degree in languages had been useful only twice in her four years with the Force. In both instances she had untangled French people with minor problems who were on a joyride over from Roscoff.

Three weeks ago she had been called in by the City of Plymouth police to investigate something "foreign." They had found a van with false number plates abandoned on Dartmoor. The only source of information was a recording machine found in a corner of the van's floor whose message was rather garbled. Two men with "German" accents seemed to be interrogating an Englishman - and it sounded nasty.

She was drawn towards two parts of the recording which actually meant something positive. "Hitler's amulet" and "Kenley airfield." She vaguely recalled recently reading of something happening in Kenley.

The Plymouth police had established that "foreigners" who had lost the use of their van and got away in a stolen ambulance had to stay somewhere. A massive search of hotels and B &B's had been made and it appeared that three men with those accents had spent one night in the New Continental. But the trail had stopped there. Completely and utterly.

The youngish hotel manager seemed more interested in Nicole's good looks and blonde hair than seriously answering her questions and Reception could only reiterate that the three men settled their bill in the normal way the morning after a one night stay. As so often happens, however, the room service lady had a little more to tell. They were desperately keen to get away, in fact near to frantic. And while she was making up the three beds one spoke very quietly to another about them getting a flight home.

Nicole moved out of the hotel into the sunshine and sat down near to the statue of Sir Francis Drake. Far out across the shining sea she could clearly see the Eddystone lighthouse. Good weather for some time to come. With luck.

Three foreigners, probably unfamiliar with the Plymouth area and maybe the whole of the United Kingdom, were stuck in the hotel after abandoning the vehicle near to Yelverton. The emergency ambulance visit to the red and green van had been requested by a voice which to her sounded very like that of the "English" guy these men had interrogated. The ambulance crew themselves had little evidence to offer, having been beaten up after cutting free the three men. All they saw were the men driving off in their stolen ambulance at great speed.

Her mind was jumping around. In order to effect such an untraceable departure from the New Continental hotel the following morning those three must surely have had help. But who would they know? And how on earth could anyone aid them? To leave the country so rapidly and escape justice they must have been assisted.

By whom? The question kept nagging away at her agile brain. Someone who lived locally? Within walking distance of the hotel perhaps? Unlikely because the red and green van they now knew had been stolen originally from the Surrey area. They were in this part of the world simply because their target was visiting here. Their help, and there almost certainly must have been some, probably came from a distance. *And therefore would have visited them by car.*

She stood up and walked across the grass and past the Smeaton lighthouse down to the small cafe. Her mind was running away with wild generalisations and she needed a strong coffee and perhaps a gateau to steady the ship. Only three people were inside. When the drink arrived she stirred in a little sugar and tried to calm herself down. But the questions kept relentlessly coming back.

When? The visit must have taken place the evening they arrived. After all they were off early the following morning.

So the car carrying their visitor would have parked in the hotel where the number plate would very likely be recorded!

No it would not!

They were dealing with skilled people able to bring about the complete disappearance of three men in ultra-quick time. He, she, or they, would not have parked anywhere where their car detail would be registered.

So it had to be *as near to the hotel entrance as possible* but in the street.

Nicole swallowed her coffee and left untouched the small roll she had chosen. A sense of excitement was beginning to well up. She recalled there were some small shops in that road adjacent to the hotel facing some of the areas where one could park. Her uniform would help get cooperation. Surely one of those places would have a security camera? It was a long shot but, these days, highly possible. She rose, settled her bill and left.

The road was buzzing with activity and the shops were busy. She took them in order of distance from the hotel entrance - nearest first. The immediate three were quick. A barber, a ladies clothing shop and a solicitor. None of them had any cctv installed. But then the fourth, an antique shop, had a man in charge who was only too keen to help. She told him she was seeking a stolen vehicle. The owner, James Dalrymple, had had his shop vandalised twice and had installed a small camera which recorded what was going on all through the night.

She gave him the date.

He came up with the pictures.

The first three cars had local registration numbers which she knew were Plymouth and West of England. But the fourth, which was only just in the camera's range had a number plate showing BX but those were the grey Jaguar's only two visible digits. The only other bit of identity which might be of use was the fairly substantial dent easily visible on the edge of the passenger door. The car slid in to the parking at 2115 and departed at 2142 hours. A quick visit taking just under half an hour - just what she would have imagined. No hanging around on a dangerous mission. The camera's range of vision went no farther but she felt it was possible that this Jaguar had something to do with the whole episode.

She thanked Mr Dalrymple, told him that probably none of the vehicles on show was the one she sought but that she may contact him again, shook him by the hand and departed.

FIFTY-FIVE

Piet was in an extraordinary mood when I called to give him the Kenley news. He almost brushed aside the information I was trying to impart to him.

"Yes, ok Dave. I am taking all of us out to lunch today. Barnaby's at one o'clock. No further questions please. We can discuss the whole thing there." He seemed so consumed by something that I hadn't the heart to bring him back a little to the real world.

"Barnaby's at one. I'll bring Elizabeth."

"Great. Jonny says he can make it if I am paying!"

I recalled that the last time Piet and I had lunched at Barnaby's he was intent on getting my IT expertise to work on a mass of papers to try to determine just where a krugerrand hike was likely to have finished up. And the weather then was awful. This time things were to be quite different.

Immediately on arrival Elizabeth saw something important - I knew from the way she moved. Women in my experience are programmed completely differently from the male of the species. They see and feel things we simply do not. She went straight to the point.

"Jessica, what a lovely ring."

The smile she got in return was stunning.

"Piet wants me to marry him. That's what this is all about."

The white sparkling wine from the Champagne region of France arrived spot on time. We toasted the happy couple, the ring and the happiness in general. But, at the same time, I could not stop my mind from wandering over the difficulties the situation would throw up. The company position of Piet? Jessica's residential problems? Where on earth would they live?

During the course of the meal the detail gradually emerged. They were going to have a small very private wedding in England and then they would move to France for permanent residence. Jessica had her old French passport and Piet would apply for French residence for as long as it took.

"And your South African job with the company?" I was somewhere between worried and annoyed as I sensed a strong negative look from Jonny. This was an inappropriate time to dwell on such a subject.

"I can still do it. I will visit regularly to carry out particular assignments as they arise. I have to go over shortly anyway to sell my place and all that, as well as for company business of course. I hope such arrangements would be acceptable?"

Jonny eyed me again. Elizabeth was more interested in other things and changed the subject fast.

"Will you go down south in France?"

"No, we will be somewhere just across the channel so that Piet can be near to you. But maybe that does not suit things Dave?" She had quickly put me right on the spot. I was thinking up an appropriate answer when my new mobile quacked. It was Giles calling from the office.

"I thought you may be interested. It's just come up on my computer. Last night two other Kenley shelters were penetrated. Doors blown as before. Nobody expected anything more like that to happen so there were no guards around. Big puzzle everywhere as to who is doing it and why."

"Thanks Giles. That is extraordinary news! We'll be back soon." I pushed the off button.

"Blighters are getting desperate. I hope we are not visited in the near future. They think we know the damned amulet's whereabouts. And they have now confirmed that I was lying. I wonder---"

My phone did another quack. It was Giles again. I put it on speakerphone so that all could hear.

"I forgot to tell you. I was playing around last night on my laptop looking at Kenley airfield. For fun really 'cos you lot seem to be in love with the place. Did you know there is another place called Kenley? It is nestled away in in Shropshire?"

We all four froze.

Thoughts instantly raced through our brains. The possibilities were enormous - or, on the other hand, completely negative.

"Good heavens no! Never thought of that. What sort of place is it?

"A small village. Rather attractive sort of place I would say."

"Giles, thank you so much." I tried to keep my voice steady. "That could be a very useful piece of information. We'll look at it when we get back."

I pocketed the phone and looked hard at Jessica. "Were you told Kenley or Kenley airfield when in Walvis Bay? Can you remember or are you not sure?"

"Kenley. Definitely just the word Kenley! Well, Kanley actually."

"We've been bloody looking at the wrong place!" Piet's impetuous character was back.

I muttered at him, "Cool it Piet. Very unlikely prisoners were kept in a small village during the war." And on that note we speedily finished our meal. A new priority had hit us with some velocity. We had to go and check.

And fast!

FIFTY-SIX

The BX number plate indicated Birmingham. Nichole's long shot assumption was that this vehicle had something to do with the three man escape. But her thinking was instantly interrupted by the latest news snippet. Two more Kenley blast pens had been blown up for no apparent reason.

Kenley again!

No mention of Hitler's amulet yet.

She simply had to go to see what was happening and put in a strong plea. A short conversation took place between her immediate boss and Kenley police and she was on her way.

The journey took nearly six hours. She felt exhausted as she pulled in to the Kenley police station where she learned immediately that an officer expert in surveillance techniques had installed a "just in case" camera after the first explosions. He was attached to the Caterham police so for him it was just a short drive.

Sergeant Cosgrove looked after her on arrival. A meal and a more or less casual discussion. It was, he said, fairly normal for them to take precautions in such a case. His camera could well have recorded something. He suggested visiting the airfield the following day but she was keen to follow through immediately despite her fatigue. He drove her there. His camera site which was across the road faced the entrance swing gate. She wandered around the bunkers and, like many others, wondered why anyone would use such force. In the meantime he thanked the house owner who had assisted him, collected his apparatus, and returned to the car where she joined him.

Back at police headquarters he ran through the pictures of the previous night's activity. Almost at midnight two cars had pulled up. Their occupants hurriedly carried a couple of bags in past the gate. Further than that there was not much to see and the car number plates very unfortunately were not visible. But then Nichole let out a small cry.

"There's a dent in the passenger door."

Cosgrove was a bit nonplussed. Maybe she had done too much travelling too quickly.

"So what?"

"I saw a groove like that on a similarly coloured Jag parked outside the hotel in Plymouth - you know, the place where the men we were looking for had stayed."

Do you have a picture?"

"I can get one. First thing tomorrow. Mr Dalrymple."

A sceptical Sergeant Cosgrove kept his feelings to himself and drove her back to the hotel for the night.

FIFTY-SEVEN

The funny thing was that the Barnaby Revelation, as we subsequently called it, was potentially so important that we returned to work each in his own way to "clear the desk." Everyone wanted to research the new Kenley and not a word was spoken for the remainder of the working day.

Elizabeth and I got down to business that evening after we had had a meal and Teddy was in bed. She projected the plan again on to the wall and I went to my computer.

"Not much about Germans in Kenley. Lots of prisoners held in various parts of Shropshire though."

"It has to be Kenley - remember?" Elizabeth as usual went straight to the point.

"Right, so we know the K beyond all doubt is for Kenley."

"Yes."

"The triangle we thought was two lines of a runway disappearing into the distance."

"Yes, but say they are not that? Could certainly be England."

"Look very closely. There is a sort of J in the triangle. Just a mark. Either faded or so weakly written you can hardly see it. What's that there for?"

Elizabeth's eyes went special branch.

"The K means Kenley. The J, if that is what it is, must stand for something in Kenley. Something, somewhere, that was there in wartime."

I stared at the screen.

"A few houses, outbuildings, farmland and not much else."

Elizabeth peered over my shoulder.

What is that?"

"Just the local church. Begins with an S."

She stared at me long and hard as if I was from another planet.

"Of course it begins with an S. Most churches are Saint something or other."

I caught the drift and brought up *Churches Kenley Shropshire.*

"Of course! St Jude's! The J! Maybe that's it! You really can't help being bright can you?"

She ignored my comments. The hunt was well and truly on.

"That triangle could be the shape of the steep roof, or England. It looks a bit like both."

I forced myself to sharpen up and think more deeply; Elizabeth was becoming really excited. "The downwards arrow leading from the amulet could mean it is down there in that hole."

"What's the HH beside the amulet mean?" My mind was now buzzing.

Elizabeth gave me one of "those" looks. The sort you feel but do not see.

"I know."

"You do? How?"

"How's your German?"

"Of course! Heil Hitler! Right beside the amulet. It *has* to be. Darling, you are brilliant."

It was my turn.

"The easy one next. A sort of square now at the bottom a St Jude's church tower rectangle?"

We said it more or less together. "The box in the ground in which the amulet is buried."

"We're there! Wait."

I had had a cool bottle of champagne hanging around for months awaiting a special occasion. I fetched it, opened and poured. We drank like two boxers just out of the ring. It had been an exhausting time but we seemed to have breakthrough. We collapsed down into two comfortable chairs to run over what we thought we had found and I tried to sum up.

"Somewhere in the St Jude's church grounds is buried the amulet we have been seeking for so long. We have to visit Kenley, Shropshire, and chat to the local vicar. Explain the situation and ask his permission to search for the amulet. Now I think we'd better tell the others. We can see if anybody else has broken through in the same way."

"OK clever clogs, but what makes you think we are there. There are two lines each side of the picture with a those circular blobs on top of them and what could be a smudged, very faint, E in the middle of one. A weak afterthought maybe. We have ignored it so far. Think that one out while I go and make a nightcap." She disappeared out to the kitchen.

I enlarged the picture of St Jude's. A graveyard which must have gone back centuries. A few trees. Grassland everywhere. Small road outside and a path leading in to the church. Nothing there to link to those lines. I was beginning to wonder if we *should* yet inform the others of our breakthrough. Would that be the best thing? They may have achieved a similar result but I doubted it. We had simply been extraordinarily lucky.

Elizabeth arrived back with two cups of hot chocolate.

"Any joy on those two balloons?"

"Nothing."

"Well forget all about them. Sometimes the mind works on these things and comes up with ideas out of the blue." She had studied psychology in the past.

And so from then on we chatted about the company, Teddy's looming junior education, my parents in law and the weather!

I awoke!

The clock showed three in the morning. Elizabeth was peacefully sleeping. All was quiet. It was those balloon shaped things that had forced me out of my slumbers. They were different. The other clues just spelt things out. We had unravelled them but this was something else. Triangle for the UK - most of it looked about that shape. K for Kenley, Shropshire. The amulet. Cross on St Jude's tower. Arrow downwards pointing to amulet small rectangular burying place. We hoped! Heil Hitler thrown in for kicks. Shakespeare – proven password.

I slipped quietly out of the bed, slid my feet into my slippers and went silently downstairs to the computer.

Up came St Jude's.

And down came Elizabeth.

"You're thinking out the reason for that balloon with a faded B – maybe not an E - and what looks like long straight lengths of string attached." She laughed. "Maybe the B is for Birthday? Anyway I promise to remain as quiet as a church mouse whilst you deliberate."

"You can have my thoughts as I go. The mind has not stopped working on all this all the time I have been sleeping. Woke up with a bit of a shock. Everything we have done so far points to the location of the amulet. But, my mind said to me, so must the balloons."

Despite her vow of silence Elizabeth breathed out one word.

"Ye-es."

"Well, what don't we know is about location?"

This time she gave a very firm response.

"The part of the church's grounds in which it is to be found. Unlikely to be immediately up against the church building."

"Exactly. So look at this picture." I quickly brought up St. Jude's on Google Earth. "How would you indicate the area in which we are to dig?" I now thought I was closing in on the answer.

She frowned. "Not the vegetation. It changes with growth or could be cut down."

I couldn't resist it. "How's your German?"

She breathed it out very slowly and thoughtfully.

"Something beginning with B or E?"

I quickly moved away from the pictures and typed in German for tree. The answer came up. It was "Baum."

"There could have been a B in each." Elizabeth leapt around the room, all promises forgotten. "We have it!"

I calmed things down and again returned to the picture of St. Jude's. "There are quite a few trees there. They look like yews. Somewhere in the depths of my mind I seem to recall that churchyards are associated with the yew tree."

"And they live for hundreds of years and are associated with death and the journey of the soul." Elizabeth knew about that sort of thing.

We both stared at the picture as I enlarged the various tree areas within the church grounds. And quite suddenly up came the solution. Two clearly old large yew trees standing about twenty feet apart. Nothing else was at all like them. I was ecstatic and rash. "That could be the complete solution! The amulet is buried somewhere between those two trees."

We went back to bed and spent the rest of the night excitedly discussing what our next move should be. Unfortunately, given the circumstance and, although I tried hard, it was impossible to get any further sleep.

FIFTY-EIGHT

The picture from Dalrymple came through the following morning. Cosgrove was delighted to confirm that the dent on the Jaguar car was in exactly the right place and looked identical to the one in his pictures.

Nichole was happy but perplexed. "We can never find that car in a place like Birmingham."

"I think it is possible."

"But the city has millions of people in it, let alone all the visitors they must get."

Cosgrove frowned. "Tell all Birmingham police officers to look for a large Jag like this, inform them of its colour and give them a picture of the dent. I'll bet that within a few days something will come up."

"It would be wonderful if they did find the car. Can the owner be interrogated on such slim evidence?"

"I would say so. Certainly some questioning. But we need to search his premises too - that could be a little more difficult - but I am sure the complexity of the case will allow for a look into his or her affairs. I'll take it from here but I'll keep in touch with you every inch of the way."

She took this as a form of dismissal but his next words put things absolutely right.

"Oh, and by the way, Nichole, *bloody well done!*"

FIFTY-NINE

Breakfast seemed like a continuation of the night's verbal exchanges. We had agreed that we had to establish whether the others had broken through as we thought we had. In the cold light of day the evidence still seemed pretty clear to us.

When Teddy arrived down I slipped away and called Jonny. No there was no conclusion there. Then Piet. He was pretty negative, I thought downcast, at the whole thing.

I said nothing.

We had decided in the early hours that if the others had had little or no joy then we should not come clean but rather that I should drive straightway to Kenley, Shropshire, and check things out. No need to involve the others if we too had been mistaken. It would be a huge disappointment. I checked the website and called the vicar of St Jude's and was lucky.

"Justin Willoughby."

"Good morning, sir. My name is David Johnston. I live in Hove and work in London. I would very much like to visit you to ask your advice on a matter relating to your church."

There was a short pause and then, "You are very welcome, David. My name is Justin. Anything in particular you wish to discuss now? If you would like a look around I will be able to meet you - say tomorrow? At the church say about midday? Does that suit?"

All else forgotten! I grabbed the opportunity.

"That would be great, Justin. Let's leave any detail until we meet. I will see you there tomorrow, and many thanks."

SIXTY

My Honda did it in about four hours.

There wasn't much to Shropshire's Kenley and I found my way to St. Jude's very easily. It was a small church building, just off the main road, looking out on to the Shropshire hills. I noted as I drove into the parking area that beyond the very historic looking gravestones there was a range of yew trees, some very large. It was twelve-fifteen and there, examining the entrance door was a five foot nine, fifties something, dog-collared, vicar. It had to be Justin.

He came towards me, hand outstretched in greeting.

"Excellent timing, David."

"The traffic was fairly light. I had an easy journey."

We walked back to the church door. "Just oiling a few hinges. This door is very old and needs attention fairly often these days. I'd like to offer you a coffee or something after your trip. Maybe at Mable's, just down the road?"

I spotted my chance.

"Does Mable do light lunches? If so are you free to be my guest? I have some tricky questions to ask, which might take some time."

He wrinkled his forehead. "Yes, could do that but I have to be back here before two o'clock. A fairly lengthy discussion I will be having about a wedding."

We strolled to my car. Mable's was a five minute drive away, a lovely small building with views out across the fields. There were three other people inside. The vicar was obviously well known and asked Mable, who had instantly appeared, for the window table away from the others. He recommended that we order her specialist omelette and fries and a couple of pints followed by coffee.

"Now, how can I help?"

"It is a long story, Justin. I'll keep it brief. Goes right back to the war." I thought I could detect somewhat more than a glimmer of interest in my problem. "Were there any German prisoners held here or in the area?"

"Not right in Kenley. But I believe some were held in Adderley Hall and Donnington. A bit before my time, of course."

"Any idea if they were let out at all?"

"No. Kept firmly under lock and key. But I do remember being told by someone that at the end of the war some worked in the fields around here before returning home. Where is this all leading anyway?"

We were short of time. The whole thing could take an hour or so explaining. I decided on the all guns blazing approach.

"We think you have buried near to your church something of great value or great horror depending on how you see it."

His eyes widened.

"Go on."

Just then the omelettes and beers arrived and we went silent. I gazed out over the fields. They certainly would not have turned down cheap German labour if it were available.

We raised glasses.

"Good to see you David."

"Great to be here, Justin. And these omelettes look really delicious."

"Local speciality." He smiled. "This little place gives us fame in some fairly elevated gastronomical circles."

There was a short silence while we did some initial justice to the meal. Then I carefully pulled out the plan and lay it before him.

"Is this what you have come about?"

Yes. I know I cannot, and do not wish, to ask you to keep secret anything untoward but can I ask for your discretion in how you handle this information?"

"Of course."

His eyes widened farther as I went on to describe what we thought was the interpretation of each symbol depicted in the picture. The food before us now took second place.

"Hitler's necklace in my church! Near some trees you say? And you want to dig it up." And then quietly, almost to himself, the words I was dreading to hear.

"Consecrated ground."

"Are the whole church grounds within the consecrated area or just part?"

"The whole graveyard and surround may not be touched!" He had become very serious.

"I saw some trees some way away. What about those?"

"Oh, the yews. That's all right - they are well away from anything. Some of them are huge and go back a century or more. They have a very interesting history."

I drew his eye back to the plan and pointed to Elizabeth's two birthday balloons. "There is a small and faint B? German Baum meaning tree."

"My goodness, you really may be on to something. But how do you know that?" Justin was becoming visibly impressed. Then he went strangely silent for a while. "Would you say an amulet like that could possibly be an instrument of evil?"

"Can a mere object give off vibes? More your line of country than mine, Justin. The amulet was supposed to have special powers but I have always doubted that."

He slowly and thoughtfully took an extra-large swig of beer. Our plates were collected and the coffee delivered. He poured unsteadily in to two cups. I helped myself to a little milk, wondering at this sudden abrupt change of atmosphere.

"You asked for my discretion. May I ask for yours?"

"Of course, Justin. Promise never to say a thing."

"This may sound mad but there has always been something going on which I have never been able to pin down. I run two churches, one successfully and then, very unsuccessfully, St. Jude's. Everything with this church has gone wrong since as far back as I can recall. The congregation, old and young, seems unusually fickle - strangely distant, if you like, from my purpose in life. The building itself suffers regularly from a range of minor structural failures. The organ fails at important moments, leading to mild chaos during times of worship. Important people, active in the church's life, get strangely sick at critical times. Electrical failures occur when no-one else seems to have them. And the list goes on. My ministry here has been hamstrung from the start - and I remember my predecessor rabbiting on about the same thing - although I thought he was exaggerating his misfortunes at the time I took over."

I grasped my chance very carefully indeed.

"So you would like it gone?"

"Well---yes. Common sense dictates that the amulet, if it is there, has nothing to do with the church's problems. However I have a strange innermost feeling about what you have told me. Sometimes things are not as they should be."

"We could arrange to look for it tomorrow. Metal detection equipment, two or three of us to work on it all day nowhere near to any consecrated ground. Then we can be gone."

"Right David. Sounds good." He looked at his watch. "If we leave now I have just time to show you exactly where you cannot go."

I waved to Mable, settled the bill, and we were off.

SIXTY-ONE

That was it! Having driven Justin back to St Jude's I went on for about half a mile to a spot where I could park and called Elizabeth.

"How are you?"

"Ok, all gone well. Much better actually than one could have expected."

"Great. What next?"

"I'll phone them direct but I would like Piet and Jonny here at St. Jude's church fairly early tomorrow morning. They should bring anything which may help in a dig which must be completed by tomorrow night."

"I am sure they will do that. Can I come?"

"We have to keep the numbers down. No extra people."

Normally I would have expected a strong discussion about this but she could hear the urgency in my voice.

"And if you find the prize, what then?"

"Considering. Not at all straightforward. I had some very interesting discussion with Justin. Will tell you all about it later."

"Right, totally understood. I will stick around here with Teddy and await events. Where are you tonight?"

"I will find a bed and breakfast or small hotel nearby. Will text where I am."

"I love you. Be careful."

"Me too. Give Teddy a kiss."

SIXTY-TWO

Elizabeth felt the situation before actually seeing it! She had just put Teddy to bed when some deep instinct caused her to glance out of the side window where, through the fading evening light, she made out two large cars moving slowly past their small house, two men in each car clearly looking for the house number.

She was instantly sure!

They had come!

Her nightmare situation. How on earth had they found the address? Dave was certain they had not once even looked at his number plate, let alone noted it down. Her own pre-arranged plan, organised purely on a flight of fancy, fell quickly to place. She rushed back in to Teddy, pulled him from his bed despite his cries, ran downstairs, grabbed her handbag, and carried him out to the garage, snatching the keys to her small IQ Toyota on the way and, at the same time, pushing the button to raise the automatic garage door. Teddy was pushed unceremoniously into the back of the car, despite his shouts, and she jumped in to the driver's seat and started up, driving quickly out and across the small road, and at the same time remembering to close the garage door. She then pulled in some twenty yards along the road between two parked cars. She showed no lights. Thankfully Teddy had become quiet, yet questioning. She told him all was well but they had to keep low down and fortunately somehow she got him to join in what he now considered to be fun. Within a couple of minutes the two sinister looking cars came crawling back and, this time with no hesitation, both pulled in to her house drive.

She had been right all along. That was why, unnoticed by David, she had removed their house number, knowing that once past her house a vehicle would have to go some way in order to turn around. And that was why she had previously planned and practised the escape route with her car which she was now following.

She was shivering with fear. These were fierce men in search of something they valued above all else. Murder and torture she knew from David was not beyond them. The Nazi curse was alive and kicking and they had her really frightened. She then called me.

"Hi Elizabeth."

"Listen! Four men in two cars are right now forcibly entering our house."

That comment shook me rigid.

"Where are you?" My voice wobbled.

"Holed up in my car a short way down the road between two other parked cars. I have Teddy in the back. I practised this getaway just in case."

"Well done. Can they actually see you?"

"Unlikely. We are well hidden. Just taking pictures of them and their cars."

I felt myself getting frantic, but knew I damned well had to control it and help her.

"Call the police - 999 straight away."

"NO! Remember we always said we had to protect Jessica."

"Oh my God. You're right. It is me they will be looking for. Oh hell, Elizabeth, just *drive away!!*"

"We know really they want detail of just where the amulet is. I suspect they will trash the place looking for clues."

"Don't even think about that. The only up to date Kenley clue is in one of those numerous atlases where I underlined Shropshire's Kenley. They won't find that. Anyway you must go now either to your mother or to the flat."

"Flat I think."

"Yes, it's the best place in the circumstances. I'll phone Piet and Jessica and tell them you are coming and explain everything. Go now! Quietly! And no stopping until you are there. Elizabeth be very, very careful! These people are the most awful fanatics."

"Right. I'm off. We can expect a wreck of a house when we get back but that really does not matter. 'Bye love."

"Goodbye my dear. See you soon."

And she was away.

SIXTY-THREE

I was staggered, shattered, baffled. I couldn't think straight.

At least Elizabeth and Teddy were safe. Something very basic was shouting at me to get a grip. The situation needed great care.

I called Piet.

Jessica answered.

"I'll keep it short, Jessica. Those thugs are ransacking my house-----"

She broke in. "Elizabeth and Teddy?"

"Escaped and ok but on their way to you for a night's lodging."

"Good. We will be ready for them. Have you told the police?" I could feel her fear. Her voice was trembling.

"No, certainly not. We ourselves can sort this out. They will not find anything in the house to guide them up here. But I think we should move fast. Got a pen?" I began to calm down as a very lame sense of responsibility tried to take over.

"Yes."

"I want Piet with all his metal detecting equipment and Jonny here at St. Jude's church by ten o'clock tomorrow morning. They must bring spades and anything which may help in a dig we must complete by tomorrow night."

"Girls stay put?"

"We have to keep the numbers down. Mustn't attract attention. And we need strong digging types."

"And if you find it, what then?"

"Considering. Not straightforward."

Piet took over from her and was straight and very positive.

"Heard it all, Dave. We'll fix everything including sandwiches and flasks of coffee. Where are you tonight?"

"I will find a small bed and breakfast nearby, failing that the car."

"Right, we will be there at ten sharp tomorrow."

"Good, that will be great if you can make it."

A final word came from Jessica. "Will text you when Elizabeth arrives."

"Super, thanks."

It took half an hour of cruising around to find a place for the night, though sleep was probably not going to be possible. Happily my phone text soon sang out.

"Elizabeth and Teddy here, safe and sound. Teddy already asleep. Elizabeth soon will be. Take care. Jessica."

At nine the following morning I arrived at the church and spent some time studying the trees. This activity seemed to have a therapeutic effect following on from a tempestuous night of self-examination. Elizabeth had been right all along. Though not pushing the point she had concluded they would find a way to track me down. Anyway she and Teddy were safe. I agreed with her. To hell with what they did to the house. I looked carefully around. There were a few yews which were surrounded by a variety bushes, but my eye was drawn to two huge very old trees that might have been set out way back when the church was built. I had learned from Elizabeth that yews could live for hundreds of years and had often been planted in churchyards, their poisonous leaves keeping off wild animals. Those two trees were about twenty yards apart and could well have been the markers shown on our plan, and maybe, with enormous luck, what we sought was put there around about the end of the war.

I surveyed the whole area in greater detail. There really was nothing anywhere near that could compete with those yews as reference points if you were going to bury something.

My thoughts were interrupted by the sound of Jonny's car which had arrived half an hour early. They must have been up in the dark, at five or even before that. I greeted them royally and indicated the best place to park, which was as near to the yews as possible. They got out and stretched, Jonny immediately pointing to the two trees."

"Maybe the target? The eye is immediately pulled towards them."

"That's what I thought. Eighty years ago or so they would still have stood out like two beacon markers."

Piet went quickly around to the boot and started unloading all the gear. I saw all sorts of horticultural gadgets which might prove useful. We picked them up and carried everything across to the tree area.

"We must clear the brush between and then start the detection work. I do somehow feel that we are in with a high chance of finding something."

"Well, Dave, let us just call it a vague bloody possibility. Then we will not be disappointed." Piet was trying hard to be the pragmatist.

"But, you know, the plan we were all trying, and failing, to decipher suddenly fell into place with the change of venue - this Kenley rather than the other one. And, sure enough, here are the two trees! We are definitely in with a chance!" I felt it important for me to keep all our spirits up at this early stage.

Without further ado we set to. It took us a couple of hours to remove the small brush and vegetation, helped enormously by a scythe which Piet had brought.

And then down came the rain.

Cats and dogs!

SIXTY-FOUR

Back in Hove events were moving rather fast. Elsie McAllister was a close friend of Elizabeth and lived only three houses away. It was her time for walking the dog while Jim stayed at home clearing things up.

As she passed Elizabeth's house she knew instantly that something was very wrong. The curtains were drawn upstairs and down and lights were on in almost every room. Elizabeth never did either of those things. There were two big cars in the drive which seemed unusual.

She took out her phone and called Elizabeth on her land line. There was no answer. Then she called her mobile. No answer.

So straightway this very intuitive lady dialled 999 and asked for the police. She told them of the suspicious cars parked outside her friend's house and how very unusual the situation was. She gave the address.

She was asked for details - make of cars, number plates, precisely how well she knew the house occupants and a variety of other questions. Unknown to her the police country-wide system automatically fed car numbers in to a specialised computer system which, before she had finished speaking, was flashing wildly, and came up asking one question. The officer put it to her.

"Ma'am is there any damage to the passenger door of the car whose registration number you first gave me please?"

She looked furtively around, saw nobody, and boldly walked her dog up the drive and around the car. "Yes officer. A dent in the door."

"Thank you. Please walk away from the area right now. Do not go near. We are on the way."

Her phone went dead.

SIXTY-FIVE

Detective Constable Nichole Sheppard was about to do an early morning departure from Kenley to return to her Devon and Cornwall police home when she heard the news from Caterham's Sergeant Cosgrove. That very day the Brighton and Hove police had arrested four men found trashing a house in Hove. The car, whose full Birmingham registration number they now had noted, had the exact dent in the offside door that she and the Caterham police had been urgently seeking. He was slightly gloating. She had not believed this rate of detection possible and he, with an extraordinary bit of luck, had been proved right.

"I'd like to go there now!"

She shouted it at her phone, knowing full well she should get the ok from her seniors back down in Devon, which well might not be forthcoming.

Cosgrove was a man who did not always follow the book. He knew a situation when he saw one. Never afraid of taking subsequent flak from his superiors he backed her.

"Go. Blame me if it all blows up but only you know anything about this whole scenario. Go. Go. Go! I will tell the Brighton force you are on the way."

It was mid-afternoon when she arrived. She was welcomed with open arms. The four men had been arrested for breaking and entering, and it was clear from the trashing of the house that the intruders were up to no good. But the Brighton police wanted more answers - and fast.

"The only connecting evidence in this whole scenario seems to be a dent in a car door." He produced a picture. "A little weak don't you think?"

Nichole, rather taken aback by this rather crude Inspector Lewis, immediately extracted from her bag a picture showing an identical dent in exactly the same place.

"Taken by a camera just off Plymouth Hoe on the night three men disappeared." She became a lot more positive. "Do your prisoners have guttural accents?"

Lewis quickly adopted a much less antagonistic attitude towards her. "No. Not at all. They seem to be a very English lot."

"Then the three rescued by the driver of this dented car have flown, probably quite literally, back to their country of origin, wherever that may be. The chambermaid in their hotel mentioned something about them talking of a flight home. My guess is that whoever owns the dented car masterminded their escape in Plymouth, learned something from them about the amulet and maybe has carried on the search. I think it pretty certain that they are a bunch of modern day Nazis and we should handle this situation very carefully."

Lewis was beginning to feel uneasy, but his disquiet was short lived. Two plain clothed men barged into the room.

He smiled. "Special Branch. I'll hand over." And with that Inspector Lewis was gone.

"Good afternoon Nichole Sheppard. I'm James Allard and my colleague here Mike Dewson. As you heard we are Special Branch Sussex police and we have been following your story at a distance."

They sat down.

She smiled. "It has all been a bit hit and miss. A bit of deep thinking on Plymouth Hoe helped."

"Can you tell us everything you know that has occurred so far? Getting to the dented car was brilliant. Without that there would be nothing to the whole affair. With it things could net us a few very nasty people."

Nichole related everything that had happened from the start and the two men seemed to hang on to her every word.

Allard looked closely at her.

"When did you last eat?"

"I had a small breakfast."

Dewsbury got the message. He went quickly out to arrange some sort of substantial tea.

"You know you've done incredibly well, Nichole. I've been able to put a few things together this morning. We went back to the neighbour who reported in about the strangeness of things where she found the dented car. The residents there are called David and Elizabeth Johnston. Their company name was given to us by the same neighbour and from this we have traced the present whereabouts of Elizabeth."

"You have been really busy." Nichole was impressed.

"Yes, sometimes we do get a move on, especially where any suggestion of Nazism is concerned."

Dewsbury arrived back with tea for three and a range of cakes for Nichole. He poured. Allard continued.

"We would like your help. Someone has to go see Elizabeth and very carefully glean as much information from her as possible. Where for example is her husband? I did not push the point when speaking to their office. Why was it *their* house in Hove which was being searched? What on earth is it that they know that brought the dented car to them? We need full detail, not just the idea of an amulet."

"And I am just the person to speak with her?"

"Yes. Better than a couple of hoary old men! And you know more about this whole thing than anybody else."

"Where is Elizabeth now?"

Allard pulled a small card from his pocket.

"Her name, addresses, phones - all on there. Also my mobile. Tackle it as only you know best. Transport is laid on and will stay with you for as long as necessary. We'll pick up all hotel bills, meals etc. Just feed us as much detail as you can, particularly any Nazi part of the story. We will deal with the four suspects who are presently saying nothing.

"Will you also talk with my masters in Devon and Cornwall?"

"Already done. They are very supportive." He smiled.

She returned the look. Special Branch had clearly left no stone unturned.

She munched happily at her second cup cake.

SIXTY-SIX

We worked on through the rain which was now sheeting down. There was a realisation that time was limited. You cannot go digging in a churchyard without some local churchgoer becoming aggressively interested.

With the ground cleared between the two yews Piet started using the metal detection equipment, the slashing rain making things more difficult. There was nothing. Two thirds of the way across from one tree to the other there was still nothing. I began to think that if anything was there it was deeper than the two feet which was the limit of his equipment.

And then suddenly Piet stopped, listened carefully, and put down a stick marker. He kept straining to hear the signal against the slashing noise of the rain. "Yep, there's a metallic item down there. Probably an old tin can or something like that."

He moved away, leaving room for a soaking Jonny to gently move the rapidly softening soil away from that spot. Gradually he dug down. I think I was more hopeful than the other two. At about the two foot mark his spade struck something hard.

We all tensed.

"How are things going?" It was Justin.

We hadn't noticed his sudden arrival. His cloak protected him from the elements but he was still just showing his dog collar. I decided to be pretty negative just now but an excited Jonny, who had learned from me that Justin was sympathetic towards our cause, ruined that approach.

"Just touched something interesting. You never know."

We all peered anxiously at the spade working methodically away. Eventually, after much careful feeling around Jonny bent down and lifted up a small metal container about the size of a large glasses case. Mud clung to it, encrusted there over many years. Washed by the heavy rain we were slowly able to remove most of it.

I noticed that Justin had become noticeably edgy. I was the only one present who knew how he felt. Occasionally in his dealings with exorcism he was aware of evil powers and, as he had explained to me, there was something, somewhere, affecting the normal running of this church. For him we might be entering a fight between Good and Evil. Because of this he was, of course, all for finding out.

"We can shelter in the church porch. Getting that thing open may well take time."

The four of us ran in to the shelter, all eyes on what we had found. Strangely, I felt myself sharing Justin's deep nervousness. Piet and Jonny tried all ways of prising open the small case but failed. Justin produced a coin and inserted it in the small gap between lid and the main box. Gradually and unwillingly it opened, the lid remaining attached on the hinged side as the top sprang apart. We unwrapped a still spotless cloth. Tensions were rising all round.

And there, in front of us, lay Hitler's long lost amulet - gold chain, silver encrusted diamonds winking at us through the gloom of the weather. This was what it had all been about!

Piet and Jonny came near to hysterical joy at the find. Justin and I were much more restrained, each deep into his own thoughts.

"We've found it. Against all the odds." Piet was really over the moon - almost out of control! "I always thought the whole thing was a bit of a hoax. But I was totally wrong!"

Jonny could still hardly believe his eyes.

And then, unbelievably, *it* happened.

There was a loud series of crashes, the noise easily audible above the slashing noise of the rain. We rushed outside to see that the large heavy stone cross, which was affixed to the edge of the church roof, had smashed into the main structure before crashing to the ground. We stood looking on aghast. Amazingly only Justin kept his cool. He looked at me and muttered quietly so that only I could hear.

"Now you *have* to understand what I was saying about this church being unlike any other. What has just happened seems to me to be evil pressing to overcome all that is good. The cross *will* be rapidly replaced and all the damage *will* be repaired. Even now I can hardly believe such an extraordinary turn of events. Yet, in a funny way, I was half expecting something like this."

I had had previous thoughts about what I would do if we found the existence of this Nazi icon completely confirmed. After my dealings with my priestly friend I was now calm and resolute, my mind instantly accepting the challenge now presented to us.

"Don't worry, Justin, I will deal with it. Consider the awful thing gone! Completely, utterly, for ever!"

We returned to the church where I carefully re-boxed and pocketed the amulet. No way was I going to let the others come anywhere near to it. I was right about its future. At this moment their thinking was all wrong. The profit motive no longer applied.

Piet was still ecstatic. "A museum somewhere? We should make an *enormous* sum."

I was very much now in another world but tried to let nothing show. They could make life difficult for a while but I was right. "We'll see about that. I think we should all go home and speak tomorrow." I said my goodbyes to Justin, shook him by the hand and said quietly that our company would send a donation to help with repairs.

"Thanks David. Let me know how you handle the future of the amulet. I can't say how relieved I am that it is leaving here!"

"Oh, and I think mum's the word don't you?"

"Totally agreed. I'm sure that's right."

We shook hands warmly. I think we both felt a strangely deep understanding existing between us and I went to my car, speeding away in order to avoid meeting Jonny and Piet again.

I called Elizabeth who answered immediately.

"Are you all right, David?"

"Yes, all ok. And you and Teddy?"

"Recovering."

"Good. No questions please. Can you drive down to the boat tomorrow morning and get her ready to depart the moment I arrive?"

"Yes but---"

"No questions. It is really important."

"Yes sir! I can be there by ten. Ready to leave eleven. I will await your arrival."

"Thanks. I will explain everything then. We will be going out and back the same day."

"Thanks for the information." There was a slight sarcasm there from one who, of course, was skipper addressing her crew.

"Bye for now."

And I closed down.

SIXTY-SEVEN

Hilda had received the HH warning call from her husband, followed by a few words.

"Police about to pick us up. Remember!!"

That set her to work. She rapidly carried out the House Plan. Papers destroyed. Address book burned, important telephone details pocketed. Within minutes the place was clean. It was now down to her to continue the work that was necessary to find the amulet. In importance that surpassed *everything*.

Her heart moved into overdrive. As did her brain. She put together a few necessities - money, mobile, clothing, food and drink, closed down the house and bundled everything unceremoniously into her car. Must get away before the police arrive.

That night she drove steadily all the way to Hove. Alex had so far missed out. She would rectify. He said he and his team would deal with the situation if by any chance they were picked up and they would re-emerge. She knew what that meant.

The essential requirement was to find exactly where Johnston might be found and she was aware now that there was only one way to find out. Normally she would have been exhausted after such a marathon night time behind the wheel but HH meant everything. This was for the Fuhrer. All the stops had to be pulled out. No looking back. Between them, despite adversity, she and Alex would succeed!

She arrived an hour before dawn, soon found the unnumbered house and parked just down the road from it, keeping the car radio quietly on. A small drink of water and couple of biscuits was all she needed right now. Any sleep was out of the question. The early risers were beginning the day, their cars haring off to work up in Town or elsewhere. Taxis were lifting groups of people to the station and, what interested her most, was that some were going for their morning outing, running, walking or exercising their dogs.

She had made sure that she was dressed appropriately. Nothing identifiable. All modest, background, daily wear. Her plea would be that her friend Elizabeth was missing. Was there any way she could she be put in contact?

She tried the story on three likely women. Not one knew the Johnstons. Then on a man who proved quite useless to her. She sat back in the car assessing her options. They were very limited. But then, after more than an hour of more careful, unsuccessful, chatting to a variety of people, came a huge bit of luck. As the morning rush seemed to be dying down the gate of the third house along swung open. A lady came out leading her dog.

Hilda was quickly out of the car.

"Excuse me, I wonder if you could help?"

"Of course, what is the problem?" It was Elsie McAllister.

"I cannot contact Elizabeth, my sister in law, who lives just here. She won't answer her phone and now I find the house is empty."

Elsie sensed that the woman was "one of us" but nonetheless put across a check.

"What is her surname?"

"Johnston. Married to David."

"Well I have to tell you that the police have been here. Something strange happened and they dealt with it. I am sure she is all right but you could check with her office. I can only just remember the name - MarketWorld - something like that. If you can wait awhile I can ask my husband, just to be sure."

Hilda very quickly checked her mobile internet. The name came up. "No that's fine, thanks very much. I will give them a call later on."

Elsie was quite upset. "A fine old business. Nothing like that ever happens around here. And then this!"

Hilda did not wish to hang around but neither did she want to move off too fast and give the wrong impression. She exchanged a few more pleasantries and then made her way slowly back to the car, started up, and waved goodbye.

SIXTY-EIGHT

Some minutes after closing down speaking with David the phone rang again.

"Good day to you. Is that Elizabeth Johnston?"

"Yes. Who is this?"

"My name is Detective Constable Nichole Sheppard. I just wondered if I could have a few words with you. It won't take long."

"Of course. Is it anything important?" Inwardly Elizabeth was curling up.

"May I call in? Just a few questions."

"When would you like to come?"

"Right now if I may. I'm parked a couple of hundred yards away."

So she knew the Pimlico hideout. Had done the research. Must be important to her. "Yes, of course. The door will be open. See you shortly." Elizabeth sped into the other room and hissed words at Piet and Jessica.

"Police arriving here in minutes. Raincoats and out? Pub down the road. Jessica must not be seen by them. I will call you when all clear. Oh, and can you take Teddy?"

They both leapt into action, collected an unwilling Teddy, and were gone.

Minutes later in walked the Detective Constable.

"May I call you Elizabeth? I'm Nichole."

"Of course. Come on through. Have a seat."

Elizabeth was pleasantly surprised to see the harmless looking diminutive figure walking briskly towards her and lowering herself comfortably downwards. She had expected a much more dominant figure.

Nichole wasted no time. She was keen to get on with the job now that she had reached this point.

"I am actually from the Devon and Cornwall police. I came across a tricky situation and have been following up ever since. We had a problem with some people who stayed at a hotel on Plymouth Hoe and this now seems to be linked with the recent raid which was made on your house in Hove."

Elizabeth showed nothing but inwardly was questioning wildly. How did they make that link? What did they know about David? How much should she say? Must keep Jessica out of it, no matter what.

"Yes, I saw them coming and slipped out. Lucky really."

"But why your house and how were you so observant? Do you have anything special there and were you *expecting something like this to happen?*"

There was a lengthy silence. Elizabeth was coming to realise that her visitor knew a lot more about things than she was letting on. She would have to spill some beans. The police clearly knew of many of the events that had taken place.

"My husband, David, became aware of something that had been hidden in this country by a German prisoner of war and we tried to find it."

"Hitler's lost amulet. Somewhere on the Kenley airfield?"

Elizabeth again showed no emotion at these revelations. This woman really did know an awful lot about them.

"Yes that's right. How did you learn about it?"

"We unravelled a small piece of a recording we found lying on the floor of the van in which a man - presumably your husband - was interrogated."

"Yes you are quite right about that. I was always on the lookout in case there was to be any horrid follow up on his experience. And sure enough one day two large cars arrived. I knew at once. But how on earth did you link Plymouth Hoe with our Hove house?"

"Pure luck. There was a large dent in a car there which corresponded exactly with one seen by your neighbour in one of the two cars parked by your house when she reported her suspicions about things not being right there."

"That would be Elsie. Great friend."

Nichole's whole body tensed as she became very down to earth. "I think you know a lot more. Can you tell me everything about this rather unusual situation?"

"Woman to woman rather than private citizen to police?"

Nichole smiled. She understood the sisterhood thing.

"Of course, unless there is anything criminal lurking around."

"I can tell you the whole story as I know it but I can never divulge just where the original information came from. Is that a good deal with you?"

Nichole nodded her agreement.

Elizabeth then gave as much detail as she could but omitted anything about there being a second Kenley and what David was now involved in. Nichole listened attentively throughout, made no notes and committed everything to memory. She turned down an invitation to tea, and after a few friendly words and passing over her visiting card, departed back to her car.

The moment she was alone Elizabeth called Giles in the office.

"Hello Giles. I just wanted to let you know that neither David nor I will be in tomorrow. He has just called me - wants to take out the boat for some reason. So I have to go down to Brighton marina. It will be all day. Hope you can hold the fort?"

"No problem at all Elizabeth. Have a good time. But I think the rain is coming again back again."

"Thanks Giles. Yes I'm sure you're right. Thick clouds everywhere. 'Bye."

Then she confirmed with Piet that the coast was clear.

SIXTY-NINE

Hilda was exhausted.

She drove until she found an isolated parking a small way out into the country, locked the car doors, left on the radio and slept. About four hours later she awoke and immediately fed in location details of MarketWorld to her satnav and then set off to find the London road. Traffic there was as bad as or even worse than her Birmingham experiences and she stop - started for several miles, in the end driving like a robot.

But then the monotony was transformed! Her heart thumped as she listened very carefully to a flash news item confirming to her what she had anticipated might happen but feared would not.

"Four detainees have escaped police custody earlier this morning and are somewhere in the Sussex area. They are dangerous and have left behind two severely wounded officers. Details are sparse at the moment but anyone noticing anything suspicious should call 999 immediately."

That had to be Alex and his men! He had drilled into her in no uncertain terms that, if ever caught, they would find a way to escape, even resorting to all out violence if necessary. The stakes were *that* high. They would now be seeking some place to hole up and she knew Alex would have acquired a phone one way or another to call her at the earliest opportunity. Most importantly they would need a car.

It was a dark middle of the afternoon when she finally came upon the company. A lamp illuminated the name and she managed to draw up her car in the only empty space in an adjacent company parking which overlooked MarketWorld's small offices. After studying the one lighted window for some time she guessed that the sole occupant was the lone man who occasionally moved around inside. She used a small torch to consult her notes and called the number.

An agonising wait and then -

"Good evening. Giles Rathbury speaking."

"Oh good evening Mr Rathbury. I wonder if you could please help me?"

"I'll try. What can I do?"

Well I am finding it difficult to contact Elizabeth, my sister in law. Nothing really urgent but her home number is not answering."

Giles read out the Pimlico number. "I think you will find her there. I was recently speaking with her."

"Thank you so much. I won't bother her tonight but will give her a call in the morning."

Giles was an open book!

"You will not find her there tomorrow. She and her husband are taking out the boat for the day." And he gave her Elizabeth's mobile number.

Hilda thought very quickly. "That's their boat down on the south coast isn't it? I've forgotten its name."

"Yes that's right, in Brighton Marina, name of Thor."

"Thank you so much. I am very pleased to learn she is well. Goodbye Mr Rathbury."

"Goodbye and good luck."

Hilda sat back, elated but exhausted with the effort, and started to think about where she should spend the night. Why on earth would they be going out in a boat at this time of the year? And in such awful weather? She dozed off - one of those catnaps to which she was prone. Just ten minutes later her buzzing phone instantly brought her to life.

"Hello."

"Alex." He sounded dreadful.

"I heard the news. Are you ok? Where are you?"

"Some gardens somewhere near the Brighton Pavilion I think. We're freezing cold, bloody penniless and the rain is threatening. We cannot get in anywhere. By now they will all be looking for us."

"Right. Listen carefully. I'm in London. I will drive down to you. Make your way to the pier and stay hidden near to it. I will park my car in the road to the west side of the pier, as close as I can manage. We can just about get four in and it will be warm. On the way down I will make a very short stop to buy food and drink. Should be with you in approximately two hours. Call me if we need to talk. I have learned a lot and will explain when we meet."

"Understood. We will find the pier and stay on the beach as you suggest. I will watch out for your car."

"On my way. 'Bye love. Be very careful."

Two hours it was.

Through the foulest weather Hilda drove fast but carefully, mindful of the disastrous effect to Alex and his men of her being had for speeding by some alert policeman. She pulled up on the west side of the pier. Within a couple of minutes Alex slid into the car beside her and slammed the door shut. He was followed shortly by the other three men who eased themselves in to a rear seating arrangement meant for two. They were all shivering and thoroughly drenched by the now pouring rain. The warmth of the car and the protection from the elements was what they had been craving. Hilda knew she had to act fast on the plan she had been hatching. She drove the short distance to the Grand Hotel and parked in a small parking space in a nearby side road.

"What now?" Alex felt deeply the hopelessness of their situation.

"You have to smarten up and we are booking in."

"What there?" He pointed in the hotel's direction.

"Yes. Go high. They're less inquisitive. You and I are taking a room. Hot bath. Dry clothes. Food and sleep. I will collect your friends for the same treatment one by one once you are safely inside."

"Right, that sounds damned good." Alex straightened his soaking clothes and managed a weak smile.

Hilda gave him a comb. "Carry my small bag and my coat. You can cover a lot of the soaking wet clothing with those. And stand behind me whilst I book in." She turned to the others. "I will leave the engine running to keep you warm. Turn off if anybody shows interest. Will be back for the next man in, say, twenty minutes."

They muttered their thanks.

There was no problem booking in and within minutes they were running a hot bath. Alex hung up his wet clothes to dry, mainly around the towel rails. He allowed himself five minutes of luxury, and then joined Hilda in the bedroom dressed in the hotel bathrobe. She came straight to the point.

"Tomorrow morning you must all be ready to go to the marina, just a short distance along the road."

"Exactly why?"

There is a boat there called Thor. It will have Johnston and his wife aboard."

"Are you sure?" Despite the present situation his eyes lit up.

"Yes, certain. We must not waste time. Just accept it and I will explain later. There are two single beds here. I will bring in the others one by one. They can each in turn have a hot bath, dry their clothes and sleep two to a bed."

"And you?"

"I'll curl up in that chair. You must all get sleep. Tomorrow will be here in ten hours or so."

There was a knock at the door. Alex froze but Hilda casually answered and collected a tray full of two meals from the trolley.

"To share between four. I couldn't ask for more."

Alex ate his share. Hilda spent the next hour successfully bringing in the other three men. Half an hour after that they were all deeply asleep, warm, bathed and fed, their clothing rapidly drying. Hilda set her watch for seven in the morning, fell into the comfortable chair, and was asleep in seconds.

It was just half an hour later Alex shook her arm. He whispered the words. "Do you think Johnston will have the amulet on him?"

"Not sure. Probably not. I don't know. It is a strange situation."

"I am calling in reinforcements. If all we have to do is beat the information out of him about the amulet's whereabouts they will not be needed but it will be good to have some friends around - just in case."

"How many?"

"About ten."

Alex made the call and they both went back to sleep.

SEVENTY

Early the following morning Elizabeth left for the Brighton marina. Teddy stayed with Piet and Jessica, enjoying the certainty of being spoiled. She was ahead of the rush hour traffic and wanted to have plenty of time to prepare the boat for whatever her strangely behaving husband wanted. On arrival she parked the car and was about to walk down to where Thor was moored when she remembered they needed to replace an old chart and so made her way around the marina.

The RNLI shop was open. She made the purchase, had a quick chat to Maria whom she knew well, returned back to the ramp, walked quickly down it and at the bottom let herself in to Thor's mooring area. The boat had been tied up in a rush the last time they had returned and, once aboard, she set about making things ship shape. Five minutes in to the work and her mobile rang out.

It *had* to be David.

But it wasn't!

"Morning Elizabeth. Giles here."

"Hello Giles."

"I've been a little worried. Just thought you ought to know. Your sister in law called me yesterday. Quite concerned that she could not contact you at home. So I gave her your Pimlico number."

Elizabeth reacted frantically, but then with care. She did not have a sister in law and nobody had called her. Something really bizarre was going on? She decided not to put Giles in the picture just yet.

"Thanks Giles. Did she sound all right?"

"Yes. All well there. I did explain that you would be on the boat today."

"I'll bet she did not know where we are moored up?"

"No that's true. I told her you would be in Brighton marina."

Again Elizabeth thought quickly. Was this a conversation that was spelling huge danger? It felt very much like it.

"She doesn't know the name of the boat. Wouldn't be able to find us even if she came down here."

"She said she had forgotten the name. I told her Thor. Hope that was ok?"

"Yes, that's great. And thanks for letting me know."

" Au revoir, then Elizabeth. Enjoy the day."

"Goodbye Giles."

Elizabeth was driven into thinking wild thoughts by that call. Who on earth was this woman? She herself had just escaped huge trouble with four men in two cars. Now this? How and why had she identified their office address? And Giles? Now she, or maybe they, had found the boat and knew she was aboard today. It *must* be connected with that amulet. There *had* to be a link. If so then at some time she could expect a visit. They would be after David.

Protection! It was very necessary to act! She fumbled in her purse and extracted the Detective Inspector's phone details which she had been given. The answer was immediate.

"Nichole Sheppard."

"Elizabeth Johnston. We met recently. I am on our boat, Thor, in Brighton marina."

"How can I help?"

"A very strange phone call. I have just been informed by our office that a sister in law, whom I do not have, was given full details of where I would be today. I fear very much that this may be connected with the detail of our discussion."

"Did you know those four men have escaped custody, beaten up two police officers, and made off? Where they are we simply do not know. It is now a murder inquiry as one of the officers has just died in hospital."

"Oh my God! How awful! David is on his way down here. That woman is almost certainly connected in some way. A sort of go-between, getting information for them. It seems they will do anything to lay hands on that amulet and they are sure David knows of its whereabouts."

Nichole's mind was now racing too. Elizabeth was no fool. Her appreciation of the situation was probably accurate. What to do? How to do it? And fast.

"Elizabeth. Is your phone well charged up?"

"Yes."

"Then call me if the slightest thing happens. You may well be in line for a visit from them but I will arrange things right now so that a strong police presence will shortly be in the marina. Do not worry. Just be watchful."

"Thanks Nichole. I'll keep closely in touch." As she finished the call her phone went again. This time it was me.

"You were engaged."

"With the police. Where are you?"

"About half an hour away."

"Those men have escaped."

"I know. Heard the news."

"It is now a murder situation. One of the policemen has died. And it is very possible they know we are here today."

"Bloody hell! You are in touch with the police?"

"Yes."

I thought quickly. My intention had been to take out the boat to a deep part of the channel and fling in the wretched amulet. Have it disappear for all time. Maybe a less obvious way---

"Elizabeth, how is the sea?"

"Calm. But it is pouring with rain."

"Can you lower the dinghy, outboard and all? I want to take her out immediately I arrive."

"David. Why?"

"I have the amulet. Long story, but the bloody thing *must* be destroyed - *for ever!* No further questions at the moment."

"But you cannot ---"

"Just do it!"

"Right I will. Be very careful."

"You too." And I ended the conversation.

SEVENTY-ONE

Morning had come all too quickly but Alex had forced the others awake. Their clothes were more or less dry and between them they then consumed the largest breakfasts that Hilda could order for two people.

She wasted no time and briefed them on all she had learned from Giles Rathbury, omitting no detail. Alex was effusive in his praise but then cut it short as he realised they had to get going quickly. Approximately ten of their colleagues would be arriving in the marina and it was imperative to speak with them. Last night's calls to them had been necessarily brusque.

Finding the whereabouts of that amulet was of paramount importance and now, thanks entirely to Hilda, they were closing in on their prey. But great care would be necessary. Being sought for murder brought with it a very active police force! One by one they exited the hotel unobtrusively. It was early morning and no-one took much notice. Hilda and Alex went last and she settled their bill at Reception. The rain, which had stopped overnight, was just beginning to fall again.

Once they were all in the car Hilda drove the short distance to the marina and pulled up in the West parking area. She was to stay near to the car in case a hasty exit was required. Alex went off to find his contact man - in last night's phone conversation they had agreed to meet outside McDonalds - while the other three started a systematic search for the boat named Thor and for their recently summoned colleagues.

Brighton Marina is built like a small town. Well known shops and supermarkets, sporting facilities, a cinema, houses, lounges, grills, restaurants and bars of all kinds abound. And, of course, all possible nautical facilities are available, owners being encouraged to live on their boats. Visitors therefore are free to roam the area at all times so a few men looking around the place would not appear unusual. The ever watchful Elizabeth was fired into action as she looked up and noticed two men in completely different areas of the marina both ominously running high powered binoculars slowly across rows of boats.

She again called Nichole.

SEVENTY-TWO

On receiving Elizabeth's urgent contact with her Detective Constable Nichole Sheppard immediately called James Allard of Special Branch. He was the only person she knew who fully understood the gravity of what had happened. A situation was building and she, for once, was at a complete loss. What to do? How to do it? And fast! She explained to him all she had heard from Elizabeth. Could they deploy a considerable number of officers to the marina?

"Impossible! Most of our force has been sent to the Midlands to head off some rather nasty violence which we know is coming there. Marches of all sorts going on today - at their request we sent our people off yesterday."

"But things at the marina could get ugly. This situation might lead anywhere. We ought to have a substantial number, some armed I would say."

Allard needed no convincing about the serious nature of what was emerging. His mind rapidly analysed the situation. "The decimated local police force just now cannot really deal with this. How long do you think we've got?"

"I can only guess. Two hours at the most before they pounce. Could be a lot sooner. We do not know how many people there are involved. We do know they are ruthless and, of course, a police murder case is now involved."

"Right, leave with me."

Special Branch had a link with the army. Little was known of it generally and the contact was rarely used.

Allard called the Brigadier to whom he had an emergency line.

"Harrison speaking."

Allard, Special Branch."

"How can I help?"

"We need some military personnel, preferably armed, in Brighton marina quickly. Escaped Nazi types are after a guy on a boat. Violence expected."

Brigadier Harrison, too, recognised urgency when he heard it.

"How soon?"

"An hour or less?"

"Right, will deal. I will see what is around the area. Will then put you in touch with the officer commanding whatever comes up." Emails instantly went out to a range of military establishments in the south-east, one arriving at the desk of Captain Tony Crank, adjutant, in the headquarters of the Royal Engineers in Brompton barracks, Chatham.

"Gadzooks! We have sappers already loaded up somewhere."

Just then Colonel A.P. Smithers passed through his office.

"I think this is us, Sir." Crank showed him the email.

"Yes, maybe. Isn't there a TCV departing for the Thames? New recruits learning how to blow lock gates I think. We could re-direct. Who is in charge?"

"Lieutenant Halliday. They are leaving about now."

Smithers considered the situation for all of thirty seconds. Correct decisions had to be made. His Sandhurst days were still with him.

"*You* take it, Tony. Draw weapons for yourself and Halliday from the armoury and go straight to Brighton marina. I will find out more and will brief you during the journey. You should be there in an hour."

Crank called Halliday who was already seated up beside the driver. The truck, loaded with twenty newly recruited sappers, was waiting at the gates. Within minutes Crank came through the heavy rain, got pulled up in to the rear of the vehicle, and assumed control. He called through to the front cab.

"Lieutenant Halliday round with us please for briefing. Driver Brighton marina, and careful but fast. We have a job to do!"

SEVENTY-THREE

Royal Engineers are not trained in crowd control. Their basic function is to keep the army moving forwards or backwards. They deal with things like mines, laying them down when retreating and fixing the threat when advancing. Likewise they build bridges or blow them up depending on circumstances. Oil refineries and the like - well they are easy. They should have been on the way to a lock on the river Thames. Lieutenant Halliday, an expert on the subject, would have taught the methods used to blow the lock gates and render the river impassable to waterborne traffic.

This was, of course, now all cancelled. Captain Crank held a plan of the marina which he had quickly downloaded before leaving his office. Already the Colonel, himself in contact with the police, was briefing him on the plan of action required. The newly recruited sappers listened spellbound as real and urgent action was now needed so early in their training. Crank waited until he had full details, considered them quickly, and then shouted his message so that all could hear above the noise of the speeding vehicle.

"Four escaped Nazi sympathisers are in the marina looking for a particular boat. They have murdered a policeman and so are very dangerous. Could do it again. An unknown number of their associates - presumably Nazi types - seem to have arrived there to help. Best estimates a dozen or so. Our job is to block each road, stop all vehicles entering and turn them back. Vehicles leaving must all be thoroughly checked. How do you identify a Nazi activist? That is where you will use your instinct. They may draw a gun on you. Leave well alone if they do but mobile the vehicle registration number, make of car and any detail to me as soon as possible. Any questions?"

"Yes sir. What do we do with these people when we find them?"

"Keep them in their vehicles and take the keys. If they try and run that indicates guilt. Tackle them. Real trouble - call the Lieutenant or me. We are armed."

Using his plan he then went on to allocate two sappers to each main way in or out. Ninety minutes out of Chatham they were approaching Brighton marina.

SEVENTY-FOUR

I pulled up in the car park after a hazardous journey back from St. Jude's. Some strange power had affected my driving and there had been several near misses. Plus unusual noises coming from the gear box. Why was I not a bit surprised by that? I looked carefully around. Everything in the marina seemed normal. Business was going on as usual. I grabbed my overnight bag, made sure the boxed amulet was safely zipped up in my jacket pocket, locked the car and made my way straight down to Thor.

Elizabeth's greeting was ecstatic. The embrace was fierce.

"Thank God you are here! We have been under some sort of surveillance. Not certain if they have found our boat yet but they sure have been searching for ages."

"How do you know?"

"Binoculars scanning everywhere. And a strange call to Giles yesterday from my sister in law. He told her I would be here today and gave her the boat's name."

"You don't have a sister in law."

"Precisely. You *are* catching on really fast!"

"They're after *me*! No question. Has to be." I thought of my unforgettable confrontation down on Dartmoor. This new lot of tyrants could only be even more viciously intent on getting their hands on that amulet.

"There will be help here soon. Nichole, who is a police officer friend, is working on it."

I walked slowly and peered over the stern of the boat.

"I see you have lowered the dinghy. I am going to take her out. This damned amulet has to be put to sleep over the side and into deep water once and for all. It is the essence of evil and somehow spreads chaos in the most extraordinary way."

"But that's crazy David. It is worth a lot of money to a war museum or somewhere like that. It is just an inanimate object."

I let out some of my feelings. "It would *wreck* the whole place. It has *evil* intent. I know it is just a piece of jewellery but believe me Nazi vibes emanate from it. They are bottled up there. *It must go!"*

"They've found us." Elizabeth was peering through our boat binoculars and realised she herself was eye to eye with another viewer. Worse still the man had several other tough looking characters standing around him. One was pointing.

"They will be coming. I must call Nichole."

I was torn. They were definitely after me. And this time the new lot would be utterly ruthless in their search for the amulet. No way of escape. I *had* to go. And then I must get back in time somehow to protect Elizabeth.

Grabbing a life jacket I made my way down to the floating dinghy, forcing myself to ignore Elizabeth's protestations and the heavy rain. I removed the ropes and clipped on the engine's safety link to my pocket. The outboard started immediately and I was off. I had worked it all out during my car journey. Straight from the marina and out to the deep sea. It was calm as Elizabeth had said and I quickly put her on full throttle. I followed a course to what I knew much deeper water.

Fifteen minutes later I unzipped my pocket, pulled out the small case, opened it and extracted the amulet which I flung unceremoniously into the sea. I could swear the diamonds snarled at me as they flew through the air. The case followed the amulet. I had learned somewhere that sea water had a destructive effect on silver over a period of time. That would help with longer term destruction. Mission complete and it was now essential to move really speedily. I turned the dinghy around and through the driving rain made my way as fast as possible back to the marina. Twenty minutes later I tied back on to Thor's stern, unclipped and climbed up to Elizabeth. I found myself facing a man with a gun which was pointing straight at me. Another evil looking guy was at his side. Elizabeth was cowering in a corner, clearly terrified.

"David Johnston. The amulet. Where is it?"

"Who on earth are you and what are you talking about?" I was desperately playing for some sort of time and tried brazening things out.

"The last time you were asked this question you managed to escape from some of our colleagues who are no longer in this country. This time there will be no slackness on our part. Failure to give this information will lead to me shooting at your wife, feet first and then the legs. Now, where is the amulet?"

I thought frantically. They would do it. I had no doubt at all. And the truth would not help.

Just then Elizabeth's phone rang out.

"Answer it! Be normal and put them off. Any messing about and I shoot."

"Yes. I will make sure of that. Please do not hurt me."

"Just do it!! And put on the speaker phone. We all want to hear."

Elizabeth pushed the relevant button.

"Hello, Elizabeth Johnston speaking."

"Nichole here."

Elizabeth broke in quickly. "Oh Nichole. Very sorry but I cannot make our dinner tonight. I tried hard to find the time but David has arrived back and I have to feed him."

She was talking gobbledegook. I knew it at once. The gunman was uncertain. The conversation sounded straightforward enough but ---

Everything depended on Nichole. There was a short pause.

"That is a great shame, Elizabeth. The rest of us will go ahead with the party. So sorry you will not be there. See you soon. Goodbye."

Elizabeth turned off her mobile and then lowered it to rest beside her on the steps.

"Now, the amulet." The handgun was aimed at her ankle but the glance was towards me. "Where on Kenley airfield is it? Or have you bloody well hidden it somewhere else?"

I saw my chance to make us a little more time. I could come clean, of course, and forced a smile. "Actually you've got the wrong place. The Kenley name is a small village in Shropshire, certainly not the famous airfield."

"How do you know that?"

"We've just worked it out." I nodded at Elizabeth and she felt in a pocket for one of the several existing copies of the plan we had been mulling over for weeks. The other man pulled out his phone, no doubt checking out the internet the veracity of what I had just said. He established the truth very shortly.

"Alex, he is correct about the other Kenley."

"So what have you worked out?"

I took the plan from Elizabeth. Both men had become pensive but still very alert.

"At the top you can see a sort of triangle. That represents the UK and the K beneath it is for Kenley."

"How do you know that?" The silent accomplice spoke.

I thought quickly. They would be aware of the South Africans and Namibia.

"Someone from Africa told us."

Both of them nodded. Those words definitely rang true.

"Beneath that clearly hangs the amulet with the letters HH."

"Heil Hitler." Alex breathed out the hallowed words.

"Beneath that again is a cross and a church."

"Name of the church?" Alex moved his handgun in my direction.

"St Jude's."

"How do you know that?"

It was in that second I hit upon the glimmer of a plan. I had heard Roger, our adjacent boat neighbour and a close friend, starting up his boat engine. My mind raced ahead whilst my mouth dealt with the immediate.

"There is a small J. Very faint. Those two circles with stems that are yew trees, not shown on here so well but which are visible on the bigger proper plan up top." I pointed to the steps leading up to the fly bridge.

"Get it."

Elizabeth's face had gone a shade of green. There was no bigger plan up top or anywhere else for that matter except the same sized original which we had deposited in our bank for safekeeping. She removed her phone from the steps and I steadily climbed upwards. The other man was watching me carefully from down below. For a short time only I knew that the top half of my body would be out of his sight. I very quickly extracted my mobile from a soaking wet shirt pocket and texted Roger.

No joke. Gun thugs. Ram our dinghy hard exactly five minutes.

His mobile dinged. He read the message and turned a puzzled face towards me. I fisted the air.

Alex gave me no further time. "Back down here. Where is it?"

I looked down, now in full view to them. "Very sorry. The proper plan is not where it should be. I've been through *everything*." I looked towards Elizabeth for help and got it at once.

"I think Penelope may have taken it yesterday."

I slowly descended the stairs in true backwards fashion, leaving the mobile up top. The wet would do it no good but that was the least of my worries.

"Go on with what you were saying." For a second time gunman's accomplice spoke.

"Well there are two yew trees shown in addition to what you have in this plan. They are to one side of the churchyard and the amulet is buried between the two of them. Go and dig it up for all I care."

I daren't look at my watch so was counting the seconds as they rapidly passed. If Roger did it he would reverse out from his mooring, turn towards us and, with luck, drive hard into our dinghy, destroying it, but causing little damage to each boat.

"On this plan where are the trees?"

I pointed to their position.

"And we should dig between the two of them?" Alex was getting very positive, even excited, about things.

"Yes exactly half way."

"Right, you two inside please."

The key was inserted as usual in the cabin door and he was now going to lock us in. But four minutes were up and I heard Roger coming. He had already reversed out from his mooring. I looked sharply at Elizabeth, then at the lengthy boat hook held in place above the inner cabin door, and then at the grab handle beside her.

She frowned, not understanding.

Roger hit hard!

I held on to the side of the boat. Elizabeth automatically clutched the handle and in that moment fully understood! Land lubber Alex staggered across and hit the side of the boat with a thump, his gun sliding across the floor. I leapt at him and hit a hard blow in to the solar plexus, then kicked the gun out of the boat. He fell in agony.

Elizabeth, cottoning on just in time, grabbed the boat hook from its high up housing and hammered it down on Alex's accomplice before he could get up from the floor where he had fallen, then stood ready to deal another blow if he dared to move. As if to order I suddenly noticed a woman police officer arrive at our mooring, puffing heavily.

"Nichole!" Elizabeth screamed out the greeting.

The Detective Constable boarded the boat quickly, saw what had been going on and immediately handcuffed Alex who was still desperately struggling to get vertical. Then she carried out the same operation on the other man and looked coyly towards Elizabeth.

"Just thought the cuffs would be useful after our strange conversation. These guys here will take them away." A couple of young sappers came running up to the boat and boarded. They had obviously been briefed.

"Right you two. Up and walk!" They pushed the now visibly frightened men off the boat and shuffled them away.

"Well done with that call." Nichole was in congratulatory mood and smiled at Elizabeth. "A whole bunch of other Royal Engineers are busy picking up small groups of Nazi activists as they leave the marina. All exits are covered. You have enabled us to collect a really dangerous group of fanatics who are mad enough to murder in the cause."

She looked at our faces. Some sort of therapy was needed!

"Time now to relax. *It's all over!*" And with that off she went with a bounce in her step.

A rather dazed Roger came slowly aboard.

"Saw it all. What on earth have you two been up to? Police, the military, boat crashing. Tell me something, David!"

"A beer down below."

Settled in there we slowly told the story to our friend. Tensions unwound as stressed minds eased. We were safe. Our friends had nothing more to fear. The baddies were gone and life could now return to some

sort of normality. It seemed natural that a second beer should follow the first. Nichole was correct.
 It really was all over.

EPILOGUE

I turned off the latest weather forecast.

A week had gone by before I had time to get my mind thinking about all that had passed. I was at home alone, sat in our lounge, with some pleasant early spring sunshine shedding light across the room through a large, well situated, window. The mad rush, which life had been the past few weeks, had died down and the dishevelled state of the house had been remedied by us both.

In all they had arrested a dozen Nazi types, including, of course, the two we had had on the boat. Some of them would face long sentences, I learned that a woman called Hilda Ashton, wife of the police officer murderer, stayed at home and was untouched by any legal process.

The Royal Engineers, and Captain Crank in particular, had come through the whole thing with flying colours, the local papers highlighting their spectacular activity in helping the police by apprehending such dangerous criminals. Nationally, and internationally too, for a few days there was considerable interest in this transient Nazi revival.

Piet and Jessica, now Marguerite, had quickly moved over to Calais where she had rented a small apartment. He was to continue his African work with the company, staying with her in France for lengthy periods. Eventually he hoped to get French citizenship. He had just yesterday returned to South Africa to sell his home as well as carry out outstanding work for our company, much emphasis now being on marketing

Plymouth's Streamline Boats as well as several other accumulated projects.

Piet and Jonny had given me a hard time after learning that the amulet was beyond recovery. Both of them had been expecting us to get an exceptional pay out, probably from one of those wealthy pundits who paid fortunes for iconic bits of history. My explanations were never fully accepted but our friendships were not affected.

Our dinghy was destroyed by the impact of Roger's prompt and very decisive action but there was no substantial damage to either of our boats. A few scratch marks were easily removed. It was a small price to pay for what might otherwise have been. We are taking our boat neighbours out for a slap-up marina meal next week.

I could not forget, and would for ever be intrigued by, the goings on at St. Jude's. Our donation to help with the church reconstruction was substantially augmented by Global when they heard my story. Already all in our company have a date in three months' time to visit Justin and inspect the repair work which by then will have been finished. He insisted that we should be his guests at Mable's. I look forward to that very much. I could tell when we spoke on the phone that he had become a different man. He had relaxed. Things were now progressing normally for him. Thus far no more strange and unpredictable things were happening at St. Jude's. I was determined that never in the future would I be drawn into discussions with anybody about inanimate objects possessing powers. Justin and I just *knew* it was possible. Probably very rare. But it could and does happen.

Nichole came to say goodbye and to thank us for all the help we had given. Elizabeth reversed the situation very firmly - it was *she* who had saved *us*! Either way the very sincere feelings were mutual. Mission accomplished, she was then off back down to the South-West to resume her duties there. I felt sure that some form of promotion was waiting in the wings for this incredibly intuitive police officer.

And today was a red letter day!

For the whole week following my trip out to sea to deposit the amulet to the deep, the channel - Dover, Calais, Normandy, even as far down as Brittany - had been in a state of constant volatility, wrecking small boats and making life difficult for the larger ones. Oil tankers and container ships, plying their way through the world's busiest shipping lanes, were being thrown around like matchsticks. Even experienced and hardened fishermen could not understand. There was no apparent cause and the weather forecast people were extremely perplexed and embarrassed at getting successive forecasts so wrong! But today that had all stopped. The sea was suddenly calm and obeying all the rules.

And *I* knew why.

A WORD ABOUT AMULETS

Amulets are objects with power worn by people to bring them success and prosperity, protect themselves from negative energies, ill-luck, evil, dangerous influences or injury. They usually take the form of medallions, crosses or intersecting circles but can, indeed, be almost any shape. The word itself comes from the Latin word "amuletum" which simply means "an object which protects a person from trouble."

Throughout the ages the use of amulets has been widespread. Ancient Egypt used the Eye of Horus amongst many other symbols. Ancient Rome associated gemstones with certain gods and planets. The Near East, China, Japan and Korea all developed their own styles of amulet as did the Abrahamic religions - Jews use Solomon era ones, Christians prayer beads, cords, medals and crosses. The Philippines, India, Nepal, Sri Lanka, Bolivia - the list goes on. The whole world throughout the ages has been seeking the benefits that amulets seemed to be able to confer.

Small wonder, then, that the leader of the most fearsome and cruel regime the world had ever seen should have had bestowed on him such an opulent and meaningful amulet jewel.

Milton Keynes UK
Ingram Content Group UK Ltd.
UKHW030744040924
447871UK00004B/88

9 781835 633472